The Little Girl and the Cigarette

The Little Girl and the Cigarette

Benoît Duteurtre

Translated by Charlotte Mandell

MELVILLE HOUSE PUBLISHING
BROOKLYN, NEW YORK

Originally published in France as *La petite fille et la cigarette*
© Librairie Arthème Fayard 2005

Translated by Charlotte Mandell

Translation © 2006 Melville House Publishing

Ouvrage publié avec le soutien du Centre national du livre—ministère
français chargé de la culture. / Published with the support of the National
Center for the Book—French ministry in charge of the culture.

Melville House Publishing
145 Plymouth Street
Brooklyn, New York 11201
www.mhpbooks.com

ISBN 13: 978-1-61219-096-9

Book Design: David Konopka

Printed in Canada

2 3 4 5 6 7 8 9 10

Library of Congress Cataloging-in-Publication Data

Duteurtre, Benoît, 1960-
  [Petite fille et la cigarette. English]
  The little girl and the cigarette / Benoît Duteurtre ; translated by Charlotte
Mandell.
    p. cm.
  ISBN-13: 978-1-933633-12-1
  ISBN-10: 1-933633-12-3
  I. Mandell, Charlotte. II. Title.
PQ2664.U812P4713 2007
843'.914—dc22

                         2006101688

The Little Girl and the Cigarette

Benoît Duteurtre

I

Each of the two texts seemed indisputable... except that they led to opposite conclusions. According to Government law, the condemned man, Désiré Johnson, was acting entirely within his rights when he invoked Article 47 of the Code of Application of Punishments, which authorized him to have one last smoke before execution. Whereas on his side, Mr. Quam Lao Ching, warden of the penitentiary, strictly applied paragraph 176.b of the prison policies, which prohibited Johnson from lighting that cigarette. Added a year earlier under pressure of the Associations for Defense of Public Health, this addendum banned consumption of tobacco within the confines of the prison. Obviously, the idea of defending the health of a man condemned to death could be considered puzzling, unless you viewed it as a refinement of cruelty; but such a measure, made for the benefit of the majority, would admit no qualification. From another point of view, Article 47, although it had fallen into abeyance, unquestionably authorized the prisoner to drag on the last few puffs through which his final wish was breathed out.

Seemingly indifferent to the fate that awaited him, Désiré Johnson continued to look obstinate. In the antechamber of the execution room, a silent exchange pitted the condemned man, a tall young black man, very calm under his dreadlocks, against the director of the institution, a Vietnamese law-school graduate, recently promoted to the directorship of this ultramodern prison to ensure that a dozen capital executions were smoothly carried out there every year. The little man's body seemed taut with a keen inner agitation. The desire to fulfill his duty without making a mistake, the fear of committing an infringement of the rules, the obligation to make a decision, were all conveyed by a repetition of the same order, issued in a mechanical voice that betrayed his lack of confidence:

"I am asking you, Mr. Johnson, please, to formulate a last wish that is compatible with the policies of this prison."

Impassive in his fluorescent orange jumpsuit, his wrists chained in handcuffs, there was nothing provocative, or even insolent, about Désiré Johnson. He displayed instead the same sort of lack of concern that had so disconcerted the jurors during his trial—when he stated he had neither stabbed nor stripped that 43-year-old policeman, in an alley near his home. Full of confidence, his gaze sincere, his head held high above his strong shoulders, he had felt obliged to add: "I passed him sometimes in the street and, honestly, he was a racist asshole. If I wanted to bump someone off, I'd have picked somebody just like him!" In view of the corroborating and plentiful evidence, this ambiguous declaration had sounded like a confession; but something chivalrous in his statement drew the audience's sympathy, especially when Désiré had added: "Don't ask me to cry for this guy who harassed kids instead of helping them. Never in my life have I harmed a child!"

The court had been divided until the prosecutor reached his conclusion: Johnson was suffering from withdrawal symptoms at the time of the crime; the weapon was found under his trailer; and to crown it all, he condoned this despicable crime. He had to pay. The question of the prisoner's simplicity arose once again, though, this morning, in Quam Lao Ching's mind, exasperated by the calm with which Johnson kept tirelessly replying:

"But, Warden, it's written."

And he held out to the director of the institution a photocopy of Article 47: a few lines taken from the Code of Application of Punishment stipulating that "the condemned man could carry out, before the execution, one last wish in keeping with the customs..." The notion of "custom" was of course open to debate, but the text went on to give a few precise examples, such as: "drink a glass of alcohol, smoke a cigarette...." These indications dating back to another era authorized Désiré Johnson, half a century later, to say reassuringly, wide-eyed, "I just want to smoke a cigarette. I have the right, Sir."

To listen to this simpleton, you'd really have thought that it was a matter, for him, not of dying in a quarter of an hour, of plunging into nothingness at the prime of life, but merely of obtaining what he had a right to have: in this case, this stupid cigarette that destroys millions of human lives all over the world every year!

After eighteen executions performed without incident, Quam Lao Ching had ended up thinking of himself, not without some conceit, as a good professional; an example of precision, humanity, and efficiency in the carrying out of democratic law. Never, however, had he encountered a case like this, and, despite all his efforts, nothing in his recollections from his student days or his legal training brought him even the beginning of an answer. Indeed, the prohibition of tobacco inside the detention center had, in the beginning, given rise to a certain tension in the high security area; but the results were there: in a few months, whether they liked it or not, all prisoners had stopped smoking. In the building's ceilings, automatic smoke detectors trapped the slightest suspicious fume, and the recalcitrant few had ended up giving up the habit under threats from the other detainees, who could no longer bear the alarms going off at all hours of the day or night. Those condemned to death, also cured of tobacco addiction, no longer asked for the famous "last cigarette"; most of them didn't ask for anything, since they were too busy thinking about their death. The doctors, for their part, advised against imbibing the little glass of rum, since certain chemical reactions between alcohol and the lethal chemical that was injected could lead to unforeseeable complications at the fatal instant.

"I just want to smoke my cigarette," Johnson repeated, in an atmosphere that was becoming more and more tense among the guards and the lawyers for the prosecution and for the defense.

The place looked like an infirmary, with its walls covered in white tiles. A medical cabinet, at one side, contained various flasks and utensils. Through the half-open door, one could see, in the next room, a kind of operating table, equipped with strong straps, upon which the condemned man would soon be "operated." Two other doors, one on the left, the other on the right, opened onto the little rooms where the guests of both parties had already taken their places to observe the macabre scene, up to the last gasp of the condemned man. Unaware of the debate that was going on in the wings, these individuals patiently awaited the beginning of the spectacle, while Quam

Lao Ching, fixed in place opposite the criminal, sought to resolve the imbroglio, without discovering in himself the firmness that would allow him to make a decision. On one hand, the Code of Application of Punishments formally granted Johnson the right he claimed; on the other, the rules of the prison forbade him from doing so; and moreover, the smoke detectors made this gesture impossible, since it risked setting off a riot. To himself, the director hoped common sense would finally win the day, and that the condemned man would accept a measure that had been adopted for the good of all. Again he tried to appeal to reason.

"Mr. Johnson, you can see clearly that isn't possible. At the first sign of smoke, the alarms will go off everywhere. Be reasonable!"

Since these words did not undermine Désiré's determination, the director's voice became tinged with indignation:

"You are well aware that it's bad for everyone. If you aren't thinking of your own health, at least respect the guards' health. Nothing compels them to endure the harmful effects of your cigarette!"

In the silence that followed, he tried other cards:

"We would be happy to offer you a hamburger accompanied by a cold beer. . . . Tell us what you would like before you go, Mr. Johnson."

The condemned man's lawyer, who had also been surprised by his request, imagined that the warden would simply disregard the request and that the matter would rest there. During the entire trial, Maren Pataki, Esq., had shown that she was incapable of summoning the slightest extenuating circumstance for her client. She was surprised, however, that a criminal of such little spirit had, with such audacity, seized hold of such a novel legal problem. Across from her, the lawyer for the policeman's family had the impression of witnessing a bad farce; but he also was confident that the director would settle these last, annoying details, as was his wont.... Everyone was expecting everything to return to order when the condemned man explained, as if to convince the others of his good faith:

"It's been a year now that I've been forbidden to smoke. So I'd just like one final taste, as I have a right to."

"But that's not true!" a voice cried out. "He's making fools of us! Come on, Warden, give him his cigarette so we can execute him."

Quam Lao Ching looked helplessly at the lawyer and pointed to the smoke detector on the ceiling of the infirmary. The furious litigant demanded a quick solution. It was clear, to him, that the murderer was continuing his provocations by means of a little game meant to delay the fatal instant. To delay any longer would amount to countenancing his insolence. Trying to pull himself together, the warden turned the other way and met the gaze of Maren Pataki, the court-appointed lawyer, whose gleaming little eyes indicated a sudden determination, as if Johnson's obstinacy had just opened a door in her mediocre career. After five minutes of incomprehension, she had caught a glimpse of a new perspective, and she wasn't going to let this extraordinary occasion slip by.... In a tired voice, Quam Chao Ling tried one last time to come to a friendly arrangement:

"Are you aware, Mr. Johnson, that you are in the process of setting a deplorable example? Others will be tempted to follow you...."

His tone was fatherly. Far from entering into these subtleties, the lawyer for the victim's family burst forth:

"I demand, Mr. Chao Ling, that you proceed to the execution as planned, at the time appointed!"

He pointed to the infirmary clock, which already showed 8:50—the injections were planned for 9 o'clock exactly. There wasn't a second to lose; but the lawyer for the defense, taking an initiative to which her career had hardly prepared her, chose this moment to step forward, rigid and solemn, and proclaim:

"Obviously, Warden, we are confronted here with an unknown legal problem that forces us to delay the execution. We must at least see what the Supreme Court advises."

"Rubbish!" her opponent replied. "The appeal was rejected. The President did not pardon the condemned man. Legally, this man is already dead!"

He had the features of an intellectual, with his balding skull, his wrinkled forehead, and his glasses. He could easily have been mistaken for a social science professor, if not for this rage that was suddenly expressed:

"My God, it's unbelievable. I have a family that's waiting in the other room: the parents, the wife, the children. A broken family that's been waiting for ten years for the convulsions of this bastard so it can start mourning!"

"All I'm asking is to smoke a cigarette."

Johnson had quietly repeated his request; he seemed to want to calm his enemy down and find a solution.

"We should telephone the Supreme Court," his lawyer said, pointing to the phone on the wall—next to which, an hour earlier, the vain vigil for a presidential pardon had taken place.

Subjected to these contradictory demands, Quam Lao Ching felt keenly that he could no longer prevaricate; he also knew that his decision would, in any case, incense one of the two parties. At 8:52, he decided that the first solution presented the disadvantage of being ineluctable: if he proceeded to the execution and committed a legal error, the irreparable fault risked turning against him. If, on the contrary, he adjourned the execution, it would be easy to give satisfaction to the victims with a few hours' delay. Not being a man to deal lightly with the Code of Application of Punishments, the director was almost convinced, at 8:53, of his obligation to delay the execution. Around him, the two lawyers anxiously followed the progress of the clock hands. Quam Lao Ching was going to utter his conclusion when he was seized by one last misgiving; postponing the fatal injection just for a cigarette risked being perceived as a bad joke, with severe consequences for his career. He closed his eyes, implored divine aid, and finally, six minutes before the execution, turned his troubled face to the lawyer for the plaintiffs, and said:

"I am very sorry, sir, but the procedure must be carried out in conformity with the law, and we find ourselves faced with an insoluble question. I must consult my superiors."

"Are you saying you're going to let yourself be intimidated by this bastard?"

"I must remind you that any infringement of the legislation would play into the hands of the enemies of capital punishment."

A wave of indignation shook the lawyer:

"And how am I going to announce that to the family? Don't you think they've suffered enough?"

His impassive face had turned red; emotion made his voice crack. Anyone entering this room without knowing the facts of the problem would certainly have thought he was someone who was close to the condemned man; but Désiré Johnson had turned to Maren Pataki to ask, without the slightest arrogance:

"So, can I have my smoke?"

Overcome by a fit of rage, as if the decision he had taken authorized him to relax, the prison warden turned around, crying out:

"Not here, sir! Certainly not here! And don't think you're going to escape your fate!"

Dressed in dark colors for this day of mourning, her lips pinched beneath a tuft of neglected black hairs, the little lawyer raised her head with authority. Her cross-examinations had not been convincing; her summing up for the defense had done nothing to save the condemned man; but she had just entered the legal annals thanks to the legal void discovered by her client. Appropriating Désiré's idea, she held out the copy of Article 47, stating:

"It's up to the Supreme Court to decide."

Nothing more remained but to let the witnesses know; in their respective rooms, they were beginning to get impatient. Without the presence of the armed guards, the two parties might perhaps have come to blows. The director thought that this confrontation, at the threshold of the execution chamber, had lasted much too long. Everyone had to be evacuated and he had to try to make sense of things, in the next few hours, without confusing the camp of the accused with that of the victim; the technical detail had to be resolved, and they had to proceed finally to the execution. Turning once again to the lawyer for the plaintiffs, Quam Lao Ching said, his voice full of unctuousness:

"There is *no change*. The condemned man is still condemned. Not having been pardoned, he will be executed in as short a time as possible, I promise. But I must know what procedure to follow."

Then, turning to the guards:

"Take the condemned back to his cell!"

Johnson still seemed just as indifferent; just a little glum for not being able immediately to appease his desire for nicotine. But the director did not like the defense lawyer's smile as she allowed herself to add, as if she had just won a personal victory:

"I don't think you can send this unfortunate back to be executed so quickly. That's not how you play with the nerves of a condemned man!"

"We'll see about that!" replied her opponent.

Désiré Johnson followed his guards towards death row, in a direction that he was the first to take. As he was returning to life, all he did was mumble, as if other people were trying as hard as they could to complicate his life:

"I wasn't asking for much."

2

The bus is almost empty, as it is every night when I climb on at the first stop. A woman loaded with plastic bags has taken a seat at the back of the vehicle; a Hindu with a grey beard and a turban is standing in the middle. The bus driver shows complete indifference as I get on; he ignores the bus pass I hold out to him, as if to signify he hasn't started work yet. Until the departure time comes, in four minutes, he spends his time putting away his jacket, sorting through various personal items, and making a call on his cell phone. That all seems normal to me and I take my place, in turn, on a seat that doesn't have one facing it so that I can immerse myself in the *Liberal Telegraph*— which has a headline on the sudden fall of the stock market, occurring just after the positive economic indicators published yesterday. Go figure. However, this kind of mystery seems perfectly normal to me too.

The vehicle sets off, or rather settles into the first traffic jam of the route: the congestion on Victory Boulevard that has blocked the areas surrounding Administration City every day, ever since the emergency plan to make traffic smoother was launched. For a whole year, road construction paralyzed every-thing. After the elaborately ceremonial inauguration of the "citizen lanes" reserved for carpools, two-wheeled vehicles, rollerblades, and automobile drivers who had a special priority card (mothers, pregnant women, handicapped people, the aged…), everyone thought the city would finally "breathe more freely," to use the mayor's words. Running down the middle of the boulevards, these special lanes became a paradise for rollerbladers and bicyclists gliding along next to each other, wearing their headphones—which gives a younger image to the city, but gets in the way of the buses and taxis. On the remaining portion of the pavement (a narrow lane on each side), ordinary cars pile up in a permanent traffic jam that makes gridlock at every intersection. I can see the faces of their drivers: mostly active forty-somethings, without any privi-leges, unlike the priority citizens and the rollerbladers who seem to burst forth from the midst of the exhaust.

So I have time to read attentively the article that takes up a whole page in small print: "Why Is the Drop in Unemployment Making Stocks Fall?" From time to time, I glance out at the sidewalk where a passerby is holding a handkerchief to his nose to breathe. Then I return to my paper, almost without noticing the group of twenty or so children who get onto the bus at the next stop, herded by two female monitors. They scatter noisily down the aisle, provoking only my murmured irritation, a discreet, "Quiet, kids!" I'm the only one who can hear this, but it does me good. The bus gets underway again and calm has returned when, a minute later, I raise my eyes to discover a strange sight.

The herd of kids—girls and boys all about twelve years old, returning from a school field trip or from a well-ventilated center—has rushed to the seats, at the urging of the minders. Now they're comfortably settled from one end of the bus to the other, all wearing the same fluorescent orange hat, a badge around their necks indicating their name and address. They are wearing brand-name tracksuits, gulping down sodas, playing with Game Boys. You'd really think they felt *at home,* in *their* bus where the next people to come on will have nothing to do but hold on, standing up! Since I am observing this scene with surprise, one of the two minders gives me a nasty look. Also wearing the fluorescent hat, she seems wholly devoted to the children's cause, even if it means looking at the world around them like a conspiracy of potential aggressors. She calls out to a little girl who's still wandering down the aisle:

"Audrey, there's a seat there, next to Gordon. Take a seat, dear...."

Now all the seats are occupied. The educational assistant looks at me again, suspicious, before placing her large arm over the shoulder of a little boy with freckles. Obviously, I could suppose that the monitors have had the children sit in order to calm them down; soon they'll ask them to get up to offer their seats to the "big people".... But it is equally possible that the kids have appropriated all the seats *so that other people can't have them.* Naturally, this second hypothesis is confirmed at the next stop, then throughout the rest of the route.

Soon there's no doubt left. Solidly ensconced in their seats, the children look scornfully (or don't look at all) at the increasingly numerous adults who are crammed into the central aisle. I see the poor people climb on, holding their bus passes, tired but still confident in shared transport, happy at having ended their work day. Then I watch their faces fall as they dive into the vehicle, and they discover that all the seats are taken. The new arrivals squeeze up against the previous ones who are hanging onto the metal bars so as not to fall: I see a couple of little old people climb aboard, a few young executives glued to their phones, some salesmen, some students and, in the back, two handsome, talkative, retired ladies in their sixties, carrying packages bearing the names of large department stores. Everyone patiently braces himself as the bus speeds up and brakes while, from the seats, the twittering, boisterous noise of the schoolchildren rises up, subsiding and then drowning everything out again.

The monitors don't bat an eyelid. On the contrary, every time a new passenger comes on and packs in the others, they seem to assure themselves, in a circular glance, that the children are still well ensconced in their seats. Chosen for the protection of the little ones, they see no reason to favor older people by giving them seats. Am I the only one who can remember the distant era when children owed respect to adults? I have to note, though, that the adults, victims of such incivility, are contemplating the brood with an expression of happiness. Some of them smile and gesture to the kids to express their friendliness; the bolder ones ask them questions about what they're studying at school, their age, their first names, where they live. Everything else seems forgotten: their tired bodies, their flagging spirits, stressed out by work. The "big people" look at this assembly of children like a touching image of the renewal of the species, the survival of humanity, the future of the world, and this idea seems to sustain them in the face of the difficulties of their own situation. Faced with this wave of love, the two companions abandon their surly attitude; they proudly raise their heads to signify what luck they have to accompany the kids into the heart of this bus, like two intermediaries between the world of the big and the world of the little.

In such a context, any unpleasant remark on my part would be ill received—unless I can count on the unexpressed opinion of certain young businessmen wearing ties, deep in their cellphone conversations. What side would they be on? The bet seems risky; the slightest initiative risks changing me into a scapegoat, booed by the crowd of the friends of childhood. But, simultaneously, an irresistible civic indignation drives me to signal to the monitors that aged people are suffering, standing up, crushed in the crowd, while the schoolchildren are chewing their Coke sticks and talking about the seventh installment of *Harry Potter*.... So that I can test the general opinion, I conspicuously stretch out my neck and send irritated glares around that end up attracting the attention of the two tall sixty-year-old ladies carrying packages. As if speaking to myself, I utter these exclamations, which become more and more distinct:

"Incredible! They're just like royalty! Not one of them will stand up and give up his seat!"

Pronouncing these words, I frown visibly, to show how shocking the situation is to me. I feel that the majority will come over to my side. For a few seconds, I continue my grimaces, hoping for the support of these energetic ladies, dressed in old-fashioned clothes, who certainly had a different kind of education. The taller one stares at me, wrathful in her turn. She ends up turning around to her friend, saying, her voice a little hoarse:

"I don't know what's wrong with him. You'd think he didn't like kids!"

I've lost my cause; now I'm outdated, even by old people. It would be useless to fight more, so I decide to immerse myself again in reading my financial news, taking up the thread of the article where I had left off: "Why does the surge in economic growth translate into an increase in deficits?" Then a barking noise makes me jump:

"Your seat, sir, I'm pregnant...."

Terrified, I look up to see a young woman with a round belly who has approached and is staring at me in a very unpleasant manner. While I hastily fold up my paper, she angrily insists, drawing the attention of some of the crowd:

"With a minimum amount of courtesy, you would have gotten up!"

While I abandon my seat, I stammer that the children should have gotten up first; but as I am defending myself, I have the impression that I myself am falling back into childhood. Their lips dripping with sweets, some of the kids have turned dumbfounded eyes in my direction. They look at me as if I were a weird, coarse being, and they dive back into their games. In the back, the two women carrying packages scrutinize me, looking down their noses at me, as if I were some rude pervert.

*

Latifa says I should be careful. If I keep railing against children, I'll end up getting into trouble.

Given the place where I work and the conditions I have to put up with, it's not so easy to look at these little monsters with their self-satisfied eyes. Our mayor—who is also my boss—shows genius every time it's a question of soothing public opinion about "more equality between the sexes," "more room for bicyclists and the handicapped," "a more humane city and a more transparent management," and, naturally, "more attention paid to children." Before his triumphal election, he had added to his program a plan aiming to transform a part of Administration City, where the main services of the city have their headquarters, into a daycare center. A few months later, the whole left wing of our office building was converted into a nursery, complete with a special entrance reserved for moms and their progeny. Having to remain neutral because of my job as a municipal employee, a technical adviser for the General Services Department, I silently deplored the destruction of perfectly livable company apartments. Passing in front of the entrance to the nursery, I especially noted the honeyed tones, the human respect with which the attendants welcomed the babies, tickling their chins, patting their shoulders, then congratulating the mothers on their fine work. This attitude contrasted with their mistrustful looks when the personnel came in, when they briskly demanded to see our badges, without making the slightest effort to recognize us from one day to the next.

Encouraged by the acclamations of the press, our mayor wanted to begin his second term by pulling off another coup that would allow him to show that he was more than ever a friend of life, youth, childhood and change. Thus the town council passed the resolution of October 10, with the aim of extending the complex of nurseries and daycare centers to all the buildings in Administration City, with half the offices assigned to other municipal services. In the resolution there figured the expression "joyful cohabitation" between the personnel of the city and the younger generation, which would henceforth share the same spaces. From that date on, infants (but also older children, when there was no school) frolicked about pretty much everywhere inside the premises. The measure also served another grand project: cutting in half the number of functionaries, whose jobs would henceforth be subcontracted outside. After the garbage collectors, gardeners, and road workers, most of the office jobs were cut and transferred to the private sector to reduce waste. In this context, which was beneficial to union resistance, the transformation of workspace into playspace tended to show that the mayor's social commitment had lost none of its vigor: to fire adults suddenly would not have gone over well; to replace them with children, though, spotlighted his indefatigable attention to the defenseless, and invited us to carry out this transformation with joy. Now that the city was no longer a "welfare state" for functionaries clinging to their perquisites, the city was concentrating its resources on the little ones—by simultaneously creating several hundred jobs for educational assistants.

This way of working seemed strange to us, at first. Children and employees now all entered through the same big door—except the respective attitude of the attendants had scarcely changed: affectionate pat for the little ones; unpleasant tone to the employees, and a request to see their badges. According to a memo from the mayor's office, municipal employees were requested to offer "the best welcome possible" to the children when they met them or passed them in the hallways of Administration City and in their workspaces. In an attempt to emulate the mayor, the management of human resources found it judicious to alternate nurseries and offices in the same buildings. So, when I type up a report on my computer, I often hear the brats squealing for their mothers in the next room.

While the personnel try their best to respect certain rules of communal life, the children take it upon themselves to do whatever they like, whenever and wherever they like. It is not rare, when I go to the bathroom, to find the hall blocked by a group of kids playing marbles or hopscotch; but I must above all not disturb the cherubs, who would take advantage of that to complain to the educational assistants. All day long, staff carrying mail or reports wait patiently for the children to make way for them. Only the mayor and his assistants still have reserved areas; but that doesn't stop them from occasionally walking down a hall full of children, under the flashes of the press photographers. Originally put forward by the PR department, this new municipal plan brought the team a surge of popularity from a public delighted that a man would decide to "wander off the beaten track" to administer the city with "an audacity and sense of imagination" that breaks with the "cushy administration" of his predecessor.

Faced with this revolution, the personnel were for the most part resigned. A good half of the employees play the game openly and never come to work without some strawberry Pez to hand out. One-third of my colleagues choose indifference, or try to look blasé in the face of the inexorable rise of this infantile wave: "We can't do anything about it, that would just make things worse, so the best we can do is get used to it and do our work...." Finally, a minority, to which I belong, finds it hard to put up with this cohabitation. Many times, when the Commission meets to go over major projects, I have taken the liberty of speaking out and expressing my reservations. Without talking about the background—which has to do with politics—I emphasized the extreme practical difficulty such a confrontation entails, for all our work. Every time, the chief executive officer of General Services and the mayor's assistant listened to my arguments; they even tried to reassure me, stating everything would be arranged so as not to disturb the personnel. At the last meeting, my speech seemed to make people a little annoyed. Why this obstinacy in regarding children as disturbing individuals? The mayor brought an end to the argument by reminding us that the voters had made a choice that seemed to him the best one for our city; one couldn't keep questioning it indefinitely for technical reasons. The debate was closed.

Although it might soften the hearts of a majority, the presence of children makes others' neuroses keener; the rights that children are granted and that are denied to us, the arrogance with which they have understood that from now on we are *on their turf,* all that makes us feel permanently humiliated. We avoid looking at them, refuse to answer their questions, or else thumb our noses at them. Still we have to watch out for the continual surveillance of the educational assistants, who have already found many victims. The process is always the same: a hostile attitude towards the children ends up being spotted and brought to the attention of the management, which is anxious to keep all potential danger away from the young people. In six months, a dozen suspects were—out of precautionary measures—transferred to other offices. By such methods the municipality thinks it can protect its young flock.

Such is, in brief, the hell I hope to escape every night, when I leave Administration City to go home. That is why that insignificant-seeming scene on the bus seemed so unbearable to me, as if the swarm of kids that had already spoiled my day were continuing to pursue me down the stairs, into the street, into the bus, everywhere; as if the harm were spreading to the point that it was becoming impossible to escape it since, from now on, in this country, children represent the law.

*

After climbing up Churchill Boulevard and turning at the corner of the abandoned bookstore, I enter Hydrangea Lane, a pretty little street lined with flowers where art nouveau cottages are lined up, not far from the city center. My house is all vertical lines, with its two red-brick floors, its pointed roof, and its flame-shaped windows. As I walk up the garden path, my dog rushes over and almost topples me over, leaning his paws on my stomach. His long white spaniel fur is wet (the neighbor's children must have aimed the hose at him). He runs frantically around me until I calm him down with:

"Sit, Sarko!"

I stroke his wet fur, then we both go into the pretty, modest little house (600 square feet on the ground floor, one bedroom on each floor) that I've shared for three years with Latifa. The odor of braised rabbit with herbs wafts into the entrance hall, stimulating my taste buds. My companion often spends all day in the kitchen. As she says, "I'd rather go to the super-market than the office"; and that's fine with me, since we both took a pact to live for our own pleasure, without encumbering ourselves with the slightest *kid*—except the kind she stews in a pot, with spices. That's how Latifa is: she prefers men to kids, even though, from time to time, the wish for a child gnaws at her despite my efforts to divert her from those evil thoughts.

We met at a concert of the Vienna Philharmonic. We were seated next to each other and our bodies, that day, seemed tensed in shared jubilation, absorbing this wonderful music: the Concerto for Oboe by Richard Strauss. At the intermission, we drank a glass of champagne in the lobby before we parted. A few days later, we met again by chance at a cocktail party of the Film Awards organized in the reception rooms at Administration City. She was there as a reporter for a women's journal for which she writes pieces on celebrities—without passion, but with an amused detachment. She looked more beautiful to me then than she did the first time: I loved her lanky tallness, the tallness of a young Egyptian middle-class girl who's grown too fast, the way she had of laughing at every-thing, her keen eyes, her slightly flat chest.

Latifa and I have in common a lack of ambition. My diplo-mas pointed to a brilliant ascension to the ministerial cabinets, provided I devoted the necessary amount of time to scheming. Instead of that, at the age of forty-five, I remained a modest technical adviser to the city. Latifa, with her intelligence and her charm, could have become a fashionable journalist.... We both made the same calculation: namely that with a little inheritance (which she had from her mother), my decent salary, a keen taste for life, a curiosity for art, pretty landscapes and all the good things in life, it would be possible to lead a much more interesting existence than the one that consists in tirelessly conquering ever higher positions and better salaries to pay the previous year's taxes. Epicurus said you should live for pleasure—adding that nothing brings more pleasure than a little sun and a glass of water. It is on this principle that our conjugal existence has rested for three years, devoted to making love, reading, eating excellent meals, spending a few days in a nice hotel by the sea, visiting our friends (not very many, all without children), going to concerts and movies, sleeping, cultivating our garden.

For all these reasons, Latifa concocted the rabbit in sauce, which is now simmering in the casserole while I go into the living room where my tall pretty wife is surfing the web. She is collecting a few gossip items from the fashion world, which she *might* use in an article that she *might* write... if she has the inclination and the time. She turns towards me, smiling languidly. Her light brown hair frames a face whose shadows and cheekbones always reveal something funny and animated that almost makes me forget the little nightmare on the bus.

Anyway, I don't have time to tell her about it, since it seems that she has one single idea in her head, before we have dinner—an idea that is conveyed by the question:

"Where?"

I think that we've recently done it on the kitchen table, in the grove at the back of the garden (almost in full view of the neighbors), many times in our bed—but not for a long time in the basement, next to the gas tank. There might be something nice and oily, proletarian and sweaty in that. So I invite my sweetie to the stairs and send Sarko—always ready to follow us—with a gentle little kick back to his corner.

It's only much later, that night, after we've had dinner and then played a game of chess, as we're drinking a pear brandy and smoking a cigarette, that Latifa says loudly, as if she had thought about it many times today:

"It might be good to have a child."

She sees me choke, the glass of brandy tipping into my throat. Then I give a horrified look, as horrified as if she were suggesting we spend our vacation in Las Vegas or Saint-Tropez. She knows all the questions contained in this attitude: "Why a child? So we can wipe his ass? So we can educate an ingrate? Isn't that the opposite of what we chose to do when we decided to live together?" Without giving me time to formulate these objections, she tries to give me an answer:

"Soon it will be too late for me. And I wouldn't want to regret it someday."

Does this strange need always end up tormenting women? I decide to say nothing and hold her hand instead, hoping once again that this feverish fit will soon subside.

3

"Please, photographers!"

The security guard, a heavyweight Pakistani who had a bald skull and wore a blazer and tie, was clearing the way. Using his thick arms, he pushed aside the horde of image-hunters gathered in front of the law courts, cameras in hand, flashbulbs popping, telephoto lenses obscenely huge. Never had Maren Pataki imagined that she could be such an object of interest to professional photographers. Even as a teenager, she had never had this starry-eyed girl's dream that was being fulfilled today. With astonishment, she observed the frenzy of these rodents scurrying over each other to reach their prey, determined to trample any poor soul who prevented them from carrying out *their work*—which demonstrated that this profession, like so many others, wasn't worth much. From lowering costs to restructuring news agencies, the adventure of being a reporter had given way to the impatience of a swarming, starving mob.

The fate of lawyers, along with that of a thousand other professions, was scarcely more enviable: all of them were reduced to the same exhausting, poorly paid pursuit—except for a few high-ranking jobs in business and finance. Faced with this general decline of professions, Maren felt as if she had just seized a once-in-a-lifetime opportunity, the one possibility of separating herself from the mass of court-appointed lawyers, floating in the stagnant water of the lower courts. Long years of conscientious work had led to nothing—since most of the time her clients were insolvent, their crimes petty and their guilt established (as soon as a miscarriage of justice seemed possible, a high-level department seized hold of the affair so it could get media attention out of it). Maren was also aware of her limited talent: her obvious bad luck, which seemed to condemn individuals she defended to the heaviest punishment. This explained why at thirty-four years of age her market value was almost zilch, while other lawyers of her generation had made brilliant advances into moneyed milieus. But overnight the young woman had been transformed into the protagonist in an *affair of state,* harassed by the media who begged her to make a statement. Returning through the sea of photographers, the bouncer cleared a path for her to the limousine lent by the General Tobacco Company. When she reached the vehicle, Maren Pataki turned back towards the press and said with a half-smile:

"For now, I can't say anything. Except that we are confidently awaiting the decision that the Supreme Court of Justice will hand down this afternoon."

The noise had died down. The press listened to each word of the lawyer's who, strangely, felt at ease in this privileged position. Was this from having seen how other people went about it, on the TV news? Was it inherent in every situation that confers a natural authority on you? Feeling relaxed, she was about to dive into the car when a barrage of questions burst forth again; then, interrupting her movements with perfect professionalism, at the last minute she issued a statement that she had worded carefully beforehand:

"I have requested a review of the death sentence... According to a very old legal custom, an execution that has been prevented for an unforeseen reason can be annulled by a special pardon. Before, this was called 'the hand of God.' Today, this could be an opportunity to reflect on the case history of capital punishment, and on its grey areas... And, naturally, on the particular case of Mr. Johnson first of all, whose guilt is far from established. Thank you."

With the self-confidence of those who decide when to speak and when to keep quiet, she closed the limousine door and let herself be conveyed towards the headquarters of General Tobacco Company.

Persecuted for years for their activity as dealers in death, the leaders of the multinational company had discovered, forty-eight hours earlier, the postponement of the execution of Désiré Johnson, and this event had seemed like a miracle to them: the positive sign they had given up hoping for. Although it concerned a criminal who was condemned to capital punishment, the incredible legal turn of events announced by the newspapers for once associated *tobacco* with *life* as no ad campaign had managed to do before. An individual had just been *saved by tobacco,* at least for a few days (they awaited the decision of the Court); a forgotten article of law made the cigarette into *man's best friend.* A glimmer of hope appeared for an entire threatened economic network.

Just after the postponement of the execution, Maren had alerted the news agencies, and the affair had spread in a few hours. At noon, the media had gathered in front of the prison to report the event. At 4 PM, the PR department of the General Tobacco Company had offered to place considerable means at the lawyer's disposal so that she could prepare her legal counterattack: an office of her own, an initial payment of 30,000 eurollars for expenses, and a company car.

The morning papers were spread out on the rear seat. Maren read one headline, then another. Almost all of them announced the affair on the front page, but it wasn't easy to make sense of them, with all the different points of view, many of them contradictory:

"When Anti-Smoking Saves a Murderer," read the *Daily Mirror,* a somewhat reactionary populist paper. For its editorialist, the smoking ban that was extended throughout the country—even in private apartments, inside non-smoking apartment buildings—bordered on harassment, exceeding the acceptable limit in a democracy. Today we were experiencing a particularly hateful consequence, when the rules of a prison were turned to the advantage of the murderer and against avenging the victims.

This pro-tobacco point of view moved in the direction the General Tobacco Company hoped for; but it turned against the accused man and his lawyer by demanding the punishment be swiftly carried out, as soon as the condemned man had smoked his last cigarette. In a subtler way, the reporter for the *Independent Democrat* wondered about this paradox: Why protect the lungs of criminals on death row? True, the regulations imposed by the anti-smoking leagues aimed in the first place for the protection of prison personnel from passive smoking; but, from another point of view, since cigarettes are so bad for your health, they had no reason whatsoever to forbid smoking for individuals they wanted to eliminate. The anti-smoking point of view was widespread among the other commentators;

but, there again, a fault line divided those who saw an opportunity in this affair to enlarge their fight for life ("No to Tobacco, No to the Death Penalty!" the *Liberal Telegraph* ran as its headline), and the strict thinkers who demanded the prohibition of tobacco throughout the land, without any favoritism for prisoners condemned to death ("Yes to Lethal Injection, No to Cigarettes!" headed the *Republican Tribune*). According to the latter, Désiré Johnson and his lawyer were exploiting the letter of the law. Faced with this provocation, the Supreme Court of Justice should proceed to the execution without any discussion, and refuse to get involved with the subtle exegesis of out-of-date articles of law.

The limousine was climbing President Bush Avenue, which was divided by a flowering meridian. On both sides of the avenue stood elegant high-rises of stone, glass or steel, topped with signs bearing the names of famous firms. Here, every square foot was worth several months of Maren's salary; she lived downtown in a tiny apartment. Fifteen years earlier, she had still believed in political radicalism, tinted with bohemian poetry by some artist friends. Confident in the future, she had been active in a feminist group and in the Prisoners' Movement. But her calculations had turned out wrong: the instant she set aside fighting for women's rights, which seemed old-fashioned to her, more virulent girls had seized hold of the matter to track down the traces of sexism everywhere with unexpected success. Maren was more interested in the fate of prisoners condemned to death—almost all of them men of color from poor neighborhoods, condemned by their race and by their social background. But, faced with the rise of violence, the courts had taken a sudden and repressive turn approved by the media, to the point of making her fight almost archaic. Never had she managed to save one single person. The imprecision of her investigations, the mediocrity of her speeches for the defense, the clumsiness with which she examined the victims—even when there was no doubt of the murderer's guilt—all that precipitated her clients more inexorably towards the lethal injection. That is how she had come to have the nickname, among her fellow criminal lawyers, "Sudden Death." They secretly felt sorry for the defendant who sought her services, lured by her so-called "expertise" in criminal law but especially because she accepted the mediocre fees of court-appointed lawyers.

The driver stopped in front of the white marble high-rise of the General Tobacco Company. The art deco building narrowed, in stepped effect, up to the sky. The bronze cupolas on each ridge had a beautiful patina. Over the monumental entranceway, a giant sculpture covered in gold leaf represented a hand holding a cigarette from which a plume of smoke rose up, recalling the time when smoking was thought of as an elegant gesture. A bellboy opened the limousine door and Maren set her sneaker-clad feet on the red carpet; she walked under the awning towards the immense lobby where an executive from the PR department was waiting for her. They entered the elevator, which rose up to the conference room on the fifteenth floor. Surrounded by wide windows, the room looked out over the city like an observatory; around an oval table of polished wood equipped with microphones and monitors sat the Vice President and the Director of Legal Affairs, surrounded by their staff. The lawyer felt slightly dizzy: never had she thought that her place would be here, among these businessmen in search of a media coup. Would she know how to speak the language of executives, to fight for a man's life with admen? Thinking that her own social survival was also at stake, she regained her breath and chose to place her trust in the engaging smile of the Vice President in charge of Public Relations:

"Tell us, Miss..."

"Ms.!" The former militant feminist corrected.

She was going to reproach herself for this slight aggressiveness, but felt that such an order reinforced her more in her status as spokesperson for law and justice.

"Sorry! Ms. Pataki, I'd like to know what you mean to plead this afternoon, during your closed hearing with the Supreme Court. We have to...organize our communication around a clear argument."

"Yes," the Director of Legal Affairs interrupted. "Excuse me for cutting you off, François, but I think we should know what we want: between the pro-smoking and anti-smoking arguments, between the supporters and opponents of the death penalty, everyone can build any theory he likes, and you have to admit that we're floundering a little...."

A little company lawyer with glasses started speaking in turn:

"I wouldn't like to seem cynical but, from a preliminary analysis, the most reasonable claim would consist in simply asking for the application of the penal code: strict respect of the law. In other words: the condemned man is authorized to carry out his last wish, he smokes his cigarette, and they inject him!"

This point of view seemed to suit the Assistant Director of Publicity, who continued:

"For us, that would present the advantage of not entering the debate over capital punishment. We'd content ourselves with emphasizing that, in this puritanical world where anti-smoking people spread terror, a man's last wish can be, quite simply, to smoke a cigarette: a beautiful message, on an emotional register."

"Okay," someone else went on, "but...whether you like it or not, all that reinforces the symbolic criminal-tobacco-death triangle. It's not necessarily good for the cigarette market."

Maren cleared her throat and obtained silence. Her interlocutors' indecision served her purposes. Now she could speak without tripping up. By acting in too servile a way towards the General Tobacco Company, she would sell herself short; the affair would lose in the long run, in its amplitude, in its moral high ground and profitability. In a collected voice, she expounded on her point of view:

"Obviously, I can understand your concerns, and I would like to thank you for the financial support you're giving me; but it is difficult, for a lawyer, to reason along advertising lines when a man's fate is at stake. So you will understand that what I'm demanding is an outright cancellation of the execution—first of all because the law permits it; secondly, because I believe in this man's innocence."

"But he confessed!" the company lawyer replied.

"A lot of innocent people have confessed in a police station or an investigating magistrate's office."

"Okay," the Vice President said, "but please, outline the general framework, the overall vision of the affair, that we can build on."

For this special day, Maren had made an effort at elegance. She had gone to the hairdresser's and wore a strict black jacket that—although it didn't quite go with her sneakers—made her look almost credible in these negotiations. As she was about to bring up the question of capital punishment, she closed her eyes, as if she could find in herself arguments that had had a long time to develop:

"You are not unaware that many men—including innocent men—have been executed since the law of capital punishment was standardized."

The little company lawyer with glasses corrected her, with a cynical snort:

"But didn't the law of July 11 confirm the repeal of capital punishment throughout the Union?"

"You are right: as the text says, 'Capital punishment is definitively abolished. However, several member states reserve the right to apply it in certain cases.' At least it's not applicable in all the cases! Still, the fact is that Mr. Johnson, like many other men, has been definitely condemned to death."

"He killed a police officer!"

"That is one of the special cases, in fact.... Except that the day before yesterday, an extraordinary sign brought the fatal process to a halt: a simple cigarette interrupted this man's execution. Johnson is simply asking for the application of a law. We are demanding more: fair justice for the poor and the actual abolition of capital punishment. The General Tobacco Company should take over this fight as of today."

The company lawyer brought her back to reality:

"And in what way, according to you, do the poor not benefit from fair treatment before the law?"

To this caustic tone, Maren guessed the implied answer: "Because their lawyers are useless, like Maren Pataki." She almost blushed, but, taking a deep breath, decided to dodge the question. Fortunately for her, everyone was wandering off into their own thoughts. Perplexed, the Vice President wondered if the company could seriously undertake such a fight, at the risk of alienating itself from a faction of smokers. A survey taken two years earlier, on the social profile of cigarette smokers, showed that as a whole they were slightly more favorable to capital punishment than the rest of the population. It would be better to use the Johnson affair modestly, taking advantage of the simple, forceful idea of smoking "as the ultimate pleasure." From another point of view, if Maren Pataki found serious arguments to demonstrate the innocence of her client, the benefit from the affair could reflect upon the General Tobacco Company by associating the cigarette maker with saving an innocent man's life. After weighing the pros and cons, he spoke up to give his verdict:

"Listen, Ms. Pataki, I don't think our company can go along with you in the fight against the death penalty. We respect your convictions, but we prefer to launch our public opinion campaign on a more consensual theme. If the Supreme Court upholds the execution, we will defend the right to the last cigarette as a final link to this earth. A beautiful image, isn't it?"

He had turned towards the Director of Legal Affairs who nodded; then the Vice President went on:

"The important thing, for us, is that the condemned man can carry out his final wish. Let the court know we are ready to provide all necessary infrastructures, for instance a completely secure execution chamber for smokers...Still, if the Court decides to go further and allows a retrial, we can envisage lending you our support, so long as you can demonstrate Mr. Johnson's innocence."

Without waiting for the reply of the obscure lawyer to whom he was offering the chance of her life, the Vice President turned towards his collaborators and said:

"I would like everyone to agree to this."

Until the Supreme Court's decision, then, Maren Pataki would keep the means placed at her disposal by the company. She returned to her limousine and asked the chauffeur to drive her to the prison for a final meeting with Désiré Johnson. Given the turn the affair had taken in three days, the lawyer was now certain that she could obtain a spectacular result. But she mistrusted her client's behavior, his idiotic self-confidence, his spinelessness, his own uncontrollable statements. Ready to announce to him that she hoped to save his life, she wasn't very surprised to see him enter the visitor's room with a nonchalant gait, still preoccupied with the same question:

"So, can I have my smoke?"

"Mr. Johnson, it's not a question of a cigarette now; I want to obtain a retrial! You have stated that you weren't there at the time of the crime! So we have to seize our chance and fight for you."

At these words, the big Rasta seemed to become meditative. As it was during the hearings, he looked as if his personal fate interested him less than a question of logic. His eyes scrutinized the lawyer, as if he had to add a slight qualifying statement:

"It's true I didn't kill him; but that guy was still a racist bastard!"

"Please, Désiré, stop justifying this murder. That didn't help us during the trial. All crimes are hateful, even if no one deserves death for them. And because I believe in your innocence, I'm going to try to get you out of this."

"You're going to speak to the judges?"

"Yes, I'm going there now!"

"Ask them, please, if I can choose the brand of cigarette. I'd like an English one; a Benson without a filter, that blows your head off!"

He began to smile:

"With a little grass, that would be even better."

The militant abolitionist smiled in pity. There was nothing to expect from this poor boy, who was incapable of doing anything to save his skin. The lawyer would have to manage on her own. After taking her leave of Johnson, she went back to the car and asked the chauffeur to take her to the Supreme Court of Justice, where she was due at 4 PM to state her point of view.

As usual, Maren Pataki's speech for the defense was below average. Despite the opportunity this novel situation offered, despite all the arguments she had at her disposal, despite her deep conviction, she couldn't find the words to convince the legal authorities of the validity of her cause. The magistrates of the Republic listened to her with condescension, as if she were a student trying to pass a verbal exam. They thought her boring, and rejected her request to cancel the death penalty; but, almost immediately, they forgot the lawyer and entered a discussion among experts that seemed to fascinate them—or at least distract them—about the novel question posed by Désiré Johnson: *the question of the last cigarette.* What was the respective value of Article 47 and Paragraph 176 b? After several minutes, the old experts in their black robes and ermine collars plunged into this fervent debate and asked the lawyer to step out until they had reached a decision.

The discussion went on late into the night. Faced with the amplitude of the problem, the magistrates regularly asked the bailiffs to bring them copies of the legal archives that piled up on the tables: minutes of famous trials, going back to the beginnings of the Republic and even to the Roman Empire. Each of the judges took advantage of the situation to discuss his own recollections from his student days, to recall some detail of jurisprudence, some interesting case dealt with in the course of his long career. The entire evening was a competition in eloquence, while the lawyer dozed off in the antechamber on a bench, awakened every half-hour by telephone calls from the General Tobacco Company, which was awaiting the verdict. The press was still massed in front of the court, around midnight, when the president of the court appeared, surrounded by three colleagues, whose ruddy, wrinkled faces concealed a schoolboy look as they announced their decision, which was taken with a vote of seven for, four against. After a long enumeration of the reasons for their verdict, the president finally uttered his conclusion:

"The condemned man, Désiré Johnson, is thus authorized to carry out his final wish, namely: to smoke a cigarette of his choosing, which will be provided for him by the management of the penitentiary. So as not to contravene the anti-smoking arrangements legally adopted within the establishment, the management of the center will have to provide (inside or outside its walls) a smoking zone, expressly conceived for the carrying out of this final wish, without harming the health of the personnel. As soon as his final cigarette has been consumed, Désiré Johnson will receive a fatal injection as an application of the punishment that was pronounced against him."

4

Adulthood was our objective and our ideal. Childhood obeyed strict rules; during those long years, we lived like prisoners waiting for their liberation. Vacations brought a fleeting feeling of autonomy, a sudden perception of the immensity of the world, which very quickly dissipated—as soon as we went back to school—in the narrow recess yard strewn with dead leaves. When I was little, you had to be quiet, obey, work, learn, and above all be patient, waiting to be received into the world of "big people." By adolescence, this wait became more urgent, cruel, and precise. The stages came one after the other: first cigarette, first allowance, first night out, first kiss...all with that day in mind when real life would take on the official title of *coming of age.* Like all kids, I eyed this paradise where all prohibitions would disappear, where it would become possible to act and choose without asking permission (at least during the brief years that would precede marriage). Certain banal gestures seemed to us like the symbols of maturity: driving a car, going to a nightclub, buying *Playboy* at the newspaper stand. But the first of these rights was unquestionably *smoking*.... Cancer was the least of our concerns; on the contrary, movies, ads, had taught us to regard this habit as a gesture of freedom. Lighting a cigarette, holding it, exhaling the smoke: this strange skill gave those who practiced it a sophisticated, elegant, modern allure. A useless and almost esthetic object, the cigarette distinguished man from animal. By this method and a few others, we wanted to grow up, as soon as possible.

How could I have imagined that thirty or so years later the most dangerous part of my existence would consist—just like a thirteen-year-old middle-school student—in finding hidden places to have my smoke, locking myself up behind a bolted door, in premises that were well-ventilated enough so that I wouldn't be caught in the act? How could I have imagined that this liberty, having just been acquired, would disappear so soon, under the rigorous pressure of measures taken for my own protection? How could I have imagined that after these years of relative freedom, my social life was going to be translated into a *return to childhood* with its prohibitions, while children were rewarded with ever-increasing rights?

I couldn't really say how it all started, but one day adults began to want to go back to their childhood. Suddenly nothing seemed more important to them than listening to the little ones, accompanying them, holding their hands, building a world that was ideally adapted to their needs, and rediscovering the childhood that was hidden in them. The dream was turned upside-down, and the big people regarded youth as the ideal example that they would now never be able to reach: spontaneity, purity, a clear skin, good health. In the first few TV reality shows, the participants were already learning not to act like mature, responsible people; on the contrary, they willingly ended up in a kind of school to learn how to sing, dance, sleep in dormitories, bicker over trifles, then publicly ask forgiveness, giving each other a kiss. Freed of the adult obsession with ridicule, they exhibited themselves in all their simplicity for a TV audience that was itself mainly composed of kids, masters of the ad market. Childhood became society's dream, the thing that would allow it to endure its constraints, just as we endured childhood, dreaming about adulthood....

Thoughts like that are crossing my mind, this afternoon, in the fourth-floor bathroom of the municipal administration building where I've locked myself in to smoke a red Marlboro ("tar: .5 mg; nicotine: .04 mg; carbon monoxide: .5 mg."). With my pants down, I drag happily on my cigarette and breathe the warm smoke deep into my lungs before exhaling. Last week, I finally succeeded in opening this sealed window, thanks to the screwdriver hidden in my pocket. This task took me several months, at the rate of a dozen or so minutes a day: I had to remove each screw, then scrape away the wood glue inch by inch, until the upright finally gave way. The secret smoker has to choose a well-ventilated area: although these tiny toilets don't have any smoke detectors, the smoke just has to go through the door to set off the hall alarm. So I always take the time to ventilate the place well and meticulously close the window before I leave.

Up until last year, a few smoking rooms still existed in the confines of Administration City. Individuals who "die prematurely" could be found there like outlaws, after they'd braved the scornful looks of their coworkers. But, ever since the children's nursery was extended to all the premises, ever since the kids became the privileged guests of this house, there's been no more question of tolerating the slightest risk of toxic smoke. Among adults, we could still "harm the health of those around us"; we were just a sorry bunch of literature- or law-graduates, or fathers, conscientious civil servants... But as soon as the brats might be exposed for one single second to the smoke, then it's all off! General ban! Useless to insist! Smokers should instead take advantage of this opportunity to correct their vice and cure their addiction.

These measures, as you might imagine, did not soften my feelings about childhood. But they also had the result of making me regress to the pleasures of puberty. Far from having corrected my addiction, I drag on my cigarette with a secret, childlike joy, in this scarcely two-meter-square space, as I reread the warning: "Smoking during pregnancy is harmful to the health of your child." Like a naughty delinquent, I make the butt glow red and tell the regulations to go to hell. With an evil smile, I hear those brats squealing in the hallway; they won't keep me from living the way I want. And my smile is transformed into a perverse grimace when I think of the nit-picking precision of the new interior regulation that promises "offenders" will be "prosecuted." Before, they made do with a warning for anyone found smoking in a non-smoking zone; now it's a matter of punishment. But the smoke warms my bronchial tubes and I feel a base joy when I remember how the mayor looked when he announced these sanitary measures! Always first on the list of the friends of childhood, moms, grandmothers! He thinks he's transformed Administration City into a protected zone; he won't get me, and I slowly spit out my smoke into his face.

I saw him in the early afternoon, during the monthly technical update on "Quality of Life." He publicly congratulated me on my report: a rather subtle study done to shed light on the *paradoxical pollution* brought about by environmental protection. No one had foreseen this surprising phenomenon: the restriction of traffic lanes throughout the city had only aggravated the traffic jams and the pollution, of which the citizens—whom the government wanted to protect—are the first victims. In its sympathy for the municipal administration, however, the press claimed for months that cars were moving more freely, that the air was purer, that everyone was happier. Today, the statistics drawn up contradict this wishful conclusion. The government had hoped to discourage motorists by dissuasive measures; they didn't work. On the contrary, the creation of the "citizen lanes" provoked a rise in the levels of sulfur and carbon monoxide. Even the summer, which used to be quiet and clean, became a nightmare, when the entire city center is turned into a pedestrian zone, aggravating the traffic jams in the neighboring areas. In vain do people keep saying *everything's better;* everyone is suffering from this situation. That's the risk of a policy that's supposed to please the friends of nature without really antagonizing the driving constituency.

After he'd said all the good things he thought about my analysis, after even regretting that his policy of "living better together" could entrain such perverse results, the mayor expressed the wish that my report remain confidential. Then he launched into a diatribe against certain members of the media who, according to him, wait for the first opportunity to denigrate his policies. Visibly, my report had annoyed him, by raising the possibility of a change in opinion, the chance of a negative view of his policies, the threat of a malevolent perspective that would impugn his actions—after the thunderous applause extolling this man, who was guided by "obsession with honesty and the public good." Does this asshole suspect, beneath his angelic looks, that I go every day to hide in the toilets so I can freely pollute my bronchial tubes and my blood—just as he insidiously poisons the citizens of this city?

When we were leaving the technical meeting, twenty or so children were dancing in a circle in front of the conference room. Every afternoon they turn up from school, waiting for their parents to come pick them up. The porter asked us to wait till they had finished. The youth leader hummed a folk-song, accompanying herself on the tambourine. The kids— about five or six—sweetly took each other's hands; they turned and skipped as they danced, and most of the mayor's assistants (who had gone out through his private door) were frozen in place with delight before this spectacle of innocence and puri-ty. All the forty-year-olds with their glasses, all the fifty-year-olds with their bald heads, all the tie-wearing functionaries, looked blissed-out, as if everyone wanted to persuade himself that a better world was beginning, that we had a lot to learn from the little ones, that it was time to abandon our status as men so we could find, in youth, a meaning to existence:

"Did you see that little girl, how her eyes are sparkling with intelligence?"

"And that little Korean boy, look at his funny face!"

My voice rang out in a sinister tone:

"Band of old pedophiles!" I cut in, pushing aside my colleagues.

I walked down the hallway, shoving aside the group of children under the gaze of the furious porter; then I turned back, adding in a glacial tone:

"Find somewhere else for these brats, and let us do our work!"

They looked at me, concerned. The most indulgent ones supposed that I was having a bad time, some sort of marriage problem. The most perceptive thought that I hadn't taken the mayor's decision to bury my report very well. The children couldn't care less; they continued to dance to a chorus that speeded up, ending in boisterous confusion. Soon afterwards, I heard them scattering as I went into the bathroom, with my mind made up to take revenge for the work conditions that were imposed on me. I slide the bolt, lowered my pants (if someone's waiting his turn behind the door, it's better to go through the motions with your clothes, since it lends more authenticity to the whole proceeding). With the help of my screwdriver, I turned the final little screw that held the window closed and opened it over Victory Boulevard, where the cars were crawling along in a colossal traffic jam. So I took out my pack of cigarettes, grasped the tip of the poison, put the filter between my lips and leaned into the fresh air to get out my lighter and light my cigarette.

*

Other circumstances explain my phobia; they go back to the weekend, to the invitation from Latifa's brother, who wanted to show us his country house. It seemed a pleasant proposition, but we were wrong to accept it, since getting involved with a family get-together clashed with our selfishly epicurean lifestyle. Another argument pleaded for this little trip: the discovery of an undulating region with an old canal running through it. The whole idea of walking among the grapevines, and then tenderly lying down together in the meadows, had made us ignore the negative arguments—in the first place, the presence of my companion's nephews: three lowly brats who, ever since they were born, have exercised dictatorial power over their parents. My brother-in-law and his wife, however, had saved up another way of completely spoiling our bucolic expedition.

Everything began on Saturday morning. Having arrived late the night before, we had spent a delicious night in a room that smelled wonderfully of pine. Awakened by the birds, Latifa had gone downstairs about 9 o'clock to have a coffee. A little later, she had sat down in front of the fireplace to light a cigarette. Scarcely had her lighter flared than her sister-in-law came out of the kitchen, calmly explaining:

"Excuse me, we don't smoke in my house...."

This "we" seemed to include guests. She had uttered this

sentence in an annoyed tone that was trying not to sound authoritarian, but didn't brook any discussion. Knowing, however, that this prohibition would be extremely disagreeable to my companion, she added right away:

"You can do without it for a little bit, it will do you good."

Visibly, she thought she was acting for our good. Seeing Latifa's crestfallen expression, she thought she should add:

"Really, I'm just concerned with the health of my little ones; plus it's not a good example."

Annoyed, but not daring to argue with her family, Latifa had finished her cigarette alone under the porch roof, out in the cold garden, while I waxed ironic to my brother-in-law:

"You remind me of the old communists. It sounds as if the number of cigarettes you used to smoke makes you all the more severe now!"

"Not at all! Believe it or not, the smell bothers us, really! I'm sorry for you both. But it's the only little rule in this house."

This *only little rule* made for an awful ambiance from that morning on.... Obviously, I should have agreed with them, admitted that this restriction was for everybody's good; I don't smoke much anyway, so the effort wasn't all that terrible. Instead of that, I focused, with an unhealthy curiosity, on the health obsession of these individuals. And the degree of annoyance my sister-in-law felt about smoking surpassed anything I imagined. In the early afternoon we had gone up to our room, Latifa and I. The radio covered our erotic acrobatics under the wide-open window. After making love, I often feel the need for a smoke (old cliché of virility, probably stemming from the thrillers of my adolescence); I had planned everything and had discreetly brought a saucer to use as an ashtray. In my bathrobe, I was leaning out the window so as to dissipate the smell of tobacco. The youngest of the three nephews was in the garden then; he looked up and saw me in the process of making smoke rings. I waved to him in a friendly way, but he immediately went back to join his mother in the living room to tell her what he'd just seen.... Five minutes later, she began to make noises in the kitchen—just beneath our bedroom—of a series of nervous coughs, as if she were bothered by our smoke. According to the laws of physics, the smoke could not *descend* to the floor below; rather it was a signal: these unhealthy noises were addressed to us. Terrified and silent, we stayed there, lying low, like two outlaws. After a brief moment of silence, my sister-in-law ended up climbing the stairs and walking several times in front of our door, coughing more loudly. Half an hour later, when we joined the family to go for a walk, she angrily reappeared:

"Really, I asked you not to smoke in the house."

As if to support her argument, she held out to us the guilty saucer with our two black cigarette butts, crushed out.

Seemingly disgusted, she exclaimed, "How horrible!", before dumping the proof in a wastebasket. The children looked at us in turn, repeating:

"Smoking is disgusting!"

"Smoking causes cancer!"

We had become the children of this whole family. Humiliated, I almost concluded that, in these conditions, I'd rather go home; but I felt the slight pressure on my fingers of my companion, who was asking me to stay calm and try to avoid a confrontation until we got back.

We could have saved this hopeless weekend with interesting conversations. Unfortunately, during these two days, it was impossible to exchange one single word among adults, since at every meal the couple systematically seated its three offspring in the middle of the table—separating the big people so as to give the children all authority over the conversation, from the main course to the dessert. As soon as a subject came up, the eldest son (ten years old) interrupted us and told us what he had done that morning at the riding club; he was upset because one of his friends had a better Game Boy than he did; then the little sister wanted to talk about her girlfriend Jennifer. Seemingly fascinated, their parents invited them to elaborate, while the youngest one wailed into his applesauce. At other times, my brother-in-law tried to look casual and started a conversation as if this hubbub didn't disturb anyone....

Sometimes the children would go to their rooms, leaving us to piece together the beginnings of an adult conversation; but suddenly Latifa's sister-in-law would interrupt the exchange because her daughter had started to scream and she had to intervene. We stayed at the table, at a loss, in the company of the youngest one and his father, who went on feeding him.

And the progeny kept their eyes open till past midnight. Exhausted, we all went back together by the Sunday night train. During this over-long trip, the three monsters never stopped running back and forth from one end of the car to the other. They hurtled down the central aisle, colliding with passengers. They screamed with happiness, they whooped like Indians; the girl chased the boy while the baby, in diapers, stumbled behind them. And then it began again in the other direction. No let up. At the start, the parents pretended they were the only ones not to hear anything. Plunged into their books, which they weren't really reading, they thought it useless to exercise any authority over young children (given the way they raised them, authority hadn't had any results anyway). Annoyed, I looked at the other passengers, apologizing for my powerlessness. Finally, understanding that they were annoying everyone, the father or mother decided to act—each one designating the other one to take on the job. Giving their voices all possible gentleness, they asked the little ones to calm down, take a seat, and play a quiet game. The children vaguely let themselves be taken hold of, then they twisted back and forth in their parents' arms with angry squeals, slid to the floor and started running in the aisle again—the girl chasing the boy, both pursued by the baby in diapers. Fascinated by this spectacle, I saw in the kids' agitation something aggressive that seemed to be aimed explicitly at us.

*

Alone, finally alone in the second-floor bathroom, my pants down, I royally savor my cigarette. Scarcely inhaled, the smoke escapes out the wide-open window, and I think that everything isn't so bad. On my way to Administration City this morning, I had felt a cheerful, beginning-of-the-week energy. The weekend is over; I won't see Latifa's nephews again for a very long time; my little flowery house, my tender love, and even the stinking streets of the city, all these everyday things seem more preferable to me than family life. Prohibitions exist, but also human ingenuity, and no one can prevent me from smoking this cigarette, in the shelter of a locked door. The fight isn't an even one, but I can still fight. Just before, as I was going into the elevator, I had succeeded in overtaking three kids, then closing the door on their faces. The elevator was already rising while they beat against the wall, furious at having to wait five minutes before they could go up to the nursery.

In short, I'm an adult, and I live as I please. I just have to keep my calm and carry out my work with professionalism—even if it means provoking a few debates with the hierarchy, as I did just now about the traffic. If the mayor is intelligent, he'll be grateful to me for such initiatives; a man in power needs to be well-informed. I inhale another mouthful from my cigarette and think I'm pretty brilliant, in my own way. Sitting on the toilet lid, I appreciate the taste of the smoke, and this pleasure again arouses the admiration I have for my own mind, for this art of giving rise to polemics, while my colleagues are content with blind approval. My grey trousers rest on the floor with the unbuckled belt. In my boxer shorts, elbows on my knees, my cigarette between my fingers, I'd look ridiculous to anyone who wasn't taking into account the extent of my influence over the organization of this city. I inhale another drag and breathe it out the window.

At that exact instant, the door handle revolves a quarter-turn. Patronizingly, I think with scorn about this intruder who should wait for me to finish. With an added sense of provocation, I take another drag of my cigarette...but, in the next instant, astonished, *I see the door start to open.* The movement is so timid that I need some time to understand that I didn't bolt it properly. Taken by surprise, I see a tiny hand appear, then the dumbfounded face of a little five-year-old girl wearing glasses and looking at me in my cloud of smoke. Caught in the act, trapped, I think that she's just a child, I shouldn't let myself be intimidated. Wrathfully, I exclaim:

"Get out of here right now! Can't you see it's occupied!"

Instead of leaving, the little girl seems fascinated by the scene. She keeps looking at me, then utters the only observation her poor brain is capable of:

"Why did you lower your pants but not your shorts?"

"Get out!"

She insists in her reedy voice:

"You know, you're not supposed to smoke here. Because of the children's health!"

This self-confidence in reciting, at her young age, the regulation that protects her makes me feel beside myself. I want to smack her, but I'd risk being caught. Suddenly I worry about the smell of the smoke that's escaping now through the open door. In one gesture, I stand up and throw my still-lit cigarette out the window. Then after a fashion I step forward—my pants still over my shoes—begging the little girl:

"Get out of here, you stupid idiot!"

This time, I press the right button. Her little runt's face reddens, some tears appear beneath her glasses, while I furiously close the door and turn the bolt again, before tidying up the place. I open and close the window several times to make a current of air; then I get out my screwdriver and seal the window frame again, screwing in the secret screw; I spray a little "sea breeze" air spray, put my pants back on and run the tap, as if to prove I was really using the toilet. Finally I buckle my belt and leave the second-floor bathroom just like any other user.... The little girl is terrified and won't say anything. I can see her a little further on, in the hallway. She's grumbling, leaning against the wall, as if my insult had annoyed her. To reinforce the psychological pressure, I pass by her, repeating quietly, but firmly:

"Idiot!"

As a way of shutting her mouth for good.

That night, back at home, I tell the story to Latifa, who contents herself with smiling. She listens to me getting carried away, as if I had taken mad risks and run a great danger. The tone of my voice betrays the climate of anxiety and suspicion that reigns at Administration City, and my companion ends up understanding that this minuscule anecdote is secretly tormenting me, as if a threat were lying over me. To bring me back to reason, she exclaims:

"Come on, you're not going to flip out because a five-year-old kid saw you smoking in the bathroom!"

She's right. I burst out laughing, pulling my chair up to the table to enjoy a dish of scallops. My anxiety won't return till the end of the evening, when Latifa whispers to me, half asleep:

"Darling, this will surprise you, but...I think it's time to have a baby."

"A what?"

"A baby, the two of us."

"You don't think there aren't enough children as it is, dearest?"

"I'm a woman, try to understand!"

"But we promised each other...."

The monsters are everywhere. They are insinuating themselves under the doors and even into the thoughts of Latifa, who's snoring now. Annoyed, incapable of falling asleep, I light the bedside lamp and get hold of the *Liberal Telegraph* that I didn't have time to read this morning. On the front page is the scoop of the week: the decision of the Supreme Court of Justice that, finally, has authorized Désiré Johnson to smoke his last cigarette before execution. The news cheers me up a little; a gleam of hope puts my secret smoker's anxiety in its proper perspective.

5

The real danger comes from those self-confident times when I'm not afraid anymore. Timid and unsure of myself by nature, I aim cautiously at modest victories. But at the instant of fulfillment when I proudly raise my head, ridicule, crouching in the shadows, is never far from overwhelming me. I've noticed it a hundred times. Mistrust every sudden surge of confidence, every victorious feeling; resist those insinuating voices that keep telling me to stop playing my cards in such a *petty, mistrustful, modest, timid* way. These voices want to persuade me that anything is possible, and I get drunk on their venomous perfume. I proudly go forth on the path to glory, my mind made up to forget the mediocre embarrassments, and then a bucket of trash falls on my head.

I had recovered my calm Tuesday morning as I went to
Administration City, having rid myself of the anxieties of the
day before. A little girl had surprised me with a cigarette in my
mouth, so what? Was I going to sink into paranoia, I who
brought such a precious contribution to the management of
the city? I had just gained a few points in the internal hierarchy by offering the mayor an intelligent contradiction of his
own policy. His very annoyance proved this: he was beginning
to understand that he needed me. Latifa had repeated to me
this morning, at breakfast: I had to stop getting worked up
over nothing; I had opportunely put a little snot-nosed kid in
her place who had the gall to open the stall door, as I was calmly occupied in smoking and reflecting.

The problems began in the late morning, while I was sorting through press cuttings that had been set aside for several
months: a whole series of paragraphs, columns, medical briefs
indicating the increase in respiratory illnesses in our city, during the last three years. Never had these facts been looked at in
relation to the measures for the restriction of traffic and the
traffic jams these measures caused. The media wanted at all
cost to represent the mayor as an infallible man—since he had
married a black woman, adopted yellow children, made his
career on the left and then conquered the office of mayor with
the help of media attention. Each one of his decisions thus
seemed beneficial. The "citizen lanes" had brought the city a

"breath of fresh air." The newspapers were content to applaud—while still pointing out, but always on other pages, the strange increase in respiratory illnesses.

Excited by my own crosschecking, I decided to present my analysis once again to the mayor's office, with more insistence: we should anticipate a reversal of public opinion, begin a subtle about-face, think about ways to organize the traffic without increasing traffic jams. I was going over my arguments when the telephone rang.... My assistant had just received a call: the Directress of Human Resources asked if I could come see her at 3:30 PM. She didn't mention the object of this meeting, but already I could detect some good news. Increase in salary? Promotion? A bonus connected to my presentations at the last few meetings? One more step would bring me closer to the dreamed-of status of *special adviser,* a freelance consultant, freed of a work schedule and paid more than average employees, to meditate freely on the subjects that interest me. I confirmed the meeting and went to the fifth floor at 3:25 PM.

To reach the Directress' office, you have to cross the room that used to be used for official lunches, a vast dining room where one could admire the extraordinary series of ancient frescos that show the history of our city: the arrival of the English flotilla, the rebellion of 1820, the visit from the Czar.... I like these immense paintings from the end of the nineteenth century, their figurative technique that isn't very inventive but is fascinating in the perfection of detail, the drapery of the clothing, the play of light on the fortifications, the bustling crowds at the open markets.... Now, in the middle of this room that's been emptied of all its furniture and all its ornaments except for the frescos, an inflatable fortified castle was serving as shelter to twenty or so 4-6 year olds who were climbing its pink plastic walls. Dressed in overalls embroidered with hearts or teddy bears, the kids squealed, slobbered, squabbled beneath the annoyed gaze of historic characters. A few aldermen in mantles seemed to be directing a scornful gaze at the brood from their Renaissance windows. Since the two educational assistants had their backs turned, I made some of my own faces at the children; a little boy started bawling.

Satisfied, I arrived at the office of the DHR and was not very surprised—given my rank in this administration—when the young porter, instead of making me wait like an ordinary employee, asked me to enter my colleague's office right away. Engrossed in administrative notes, she raised her head, smiled perfunctorily, and screwed up her mouth to say, visibly annoyed:

"Listen, I'm pretty upset. I have to talk to you about something...weird!"

This was the rule at the mayor's office: all upper executives talked familiarly to each other, using first names. She went on:

"Something a little unhealthy...that concerns you directly."

My face fell in a dumbfounded pout, as she continued:

"I'm not going to beat round the bush. Tell me clearly: did you go to the bathroom, yesterday, with a little girl?"

My wide-open eyes expressed incredulity. Did I hear right? Bathroom? Little girl? Was this shortened version of events giving a note of perversity to the micro-event of the day before? Indignation welled up in my voice:

"You're joking, right? You don't believe I'd bring kids to the bathroom with me?"

My colleague seemed overwhelmed:

"This business bothers me terribly. Of course I don't believe anything, but...how to say it...the word of a child is at stake!"

The little girl had denounced me! I had fallen into the trap...except that after all I hadn't done anything wrong; nothing more serious than smoking a cigarette. I smelled the sudden sweatiness of my skin. At that instant I should have told her exactly what had happened; but a kind of sense of modesty drove me to deny everything. No question of portraying myself as a dirty little boy who smokes in secret in the toilet stalls. Useless to mention this cigarette; the little girl had no proof. I breathed slowly to calm myself down and then said:

"Listen, it's all very simple: yes, I went to the bathroom yesterday, after a meeting with the mayor. Yes, a little girl came in, since I hadn't bolted the door properly. Yes, I asked her to leave and I closed the door again. In offices that are invaded by children, that kind of thing can happen, can't it?

There's absolutely nothing else. We aren't going to spend all afternoon on it."

The DHR remained friendly but not really convinced. She waited a little before asking:

"Can I ask you what you were doing in the bathroom?"

What did this incongruous question mean? I shrugged my shoulders, snickering:

"Listen, I was doing what you always do in the bathroom."

"The little girl states you threw a cigarette out the window. And she also claims that you threatened her!"

The police-like precision of the interrogation contrasted with the ridiculous feebleness of the facts. As I suspected, I was thus being accused *of having smoked a cigarette.* At that instant, the simplest thing would have been to confess. But the idea of describing myself in my boxer shorts, cigarette butt in my mouth, armed with my screwdriver, had something decidedly humiliating about it. Looking for a logical answer, I said:

"Look, you know that the windows are bolted shut. Plus, all of Administration City is equipped with smoke detectors!"

"The annoying thing is, at the same time, on Victory Boulevard, a passerby had a cigarette butt hit her on the head—it had fallen from a window of this building. Suffice it to say that she is not at all happy, and she's threatening to press charges. I don't want to overwhelm you...."

Although I was tempted to avoid it, this conclusion relieved me. It even seemed as if I had been waiting for it since the beginning, since that first day when I had begun to unseal the window. There was nothing irresistible about my need to smoke; it was rather a question of a perverse wish to transgress the rules, a childlike need to be caught red-handed, reprimanded and punished.... Fine: Everyone would know that I was smoking in secret, in the toilets in Administration City. Fine: I had broken the rules; the crime was a small one. The punishment wouldn't be too severe even if, in the general context of the anti-smoking campaign, I would have to expect a delay in my promotion. Now that this recital of facts was over, I waited for the verdict of the DHR, who didn't seem to want to find a compromise:

"Listen, I don't know what to say to you, but the girl has gone and complained to her parents; you'll have to expect some punishment. Especially with that cigarette thrown out the window.... I'm going to see how to find a reasonable arrangement with your director. I promise you I'll try my best."

I gestured soberly to my colleague to thank her. Then I went home, greatly vexed by this carefully prepared failure. For years, I had tried to escape the surrounding madness, the tyrannies of the time; I didn't have a car, I didn't have children, I didn't watch TV much, I turned a deaf ear to people who wanted to protect me despite myself. For years, I had tried to forget these constraints so that I could devote myself to my work, to my love, to our gentle, guarded existence. Despite all these efforts, the surrounding madness had succeeded in trapping me. I was almost ashamed to tell Latifa how the DHR had trapped me and unmasked me, how my career was, if not compromised, then at least checked. The mayor, who mistrusted me, would have a fine time of it, retorting in the midst of a public meeting:

"Before you concern yourself with the city's pollution and the lungs of your fellow citizens, you should start by stopping smoking in the toilets!"

As I grumbled, I stroked Sarko, who seemed to want to console me, and leaned his big furry head on my legs. After I had told my story, Latifa served two aperitifs. The Count Basie Orchestra, playing on TV, almost made me think that happiness was possible, and that professional success had no importance whatsoever so long as we could both cultivate the art of living in our love nest. That night, my companion had the delicacy not to talk about babies.

*

The affair didn't cause any waves until the end of the week. I was waiting for the DHR's verdict; nothing seemed to have filtered into the municipal personnel or changed my work conditions. It wasn't till the following Monday, when I went home, that I had the nasty surprise of finding, in the mailbox, a little piece of blue paper summoning me to the police station for a hearing with the Juvenile Division.

I looked at the summons without moving. This smelled bad, very bad. As I held the missive out to her, with staring eyes, Latifa was silent; but what really made me panic was the energetic tone with which she suddenly announced—as if she were standing up for a lost cause:

"We'll fight!"

Fight against what? Because it was understood that I had smoked a cigarette in secret; I was ready to pay for having overstepped the rules, placed the children's health in danger, and almost set off the fire alarms. What else did they want? I accepted my guilt and its administrative consequences en bloc, but the unforeseen shift from the company's human resource department to the Criminal Investigation Department was unsettling, and I spent hours going over the various hypotheses: had the little girl's parents mobilized other parents, convinced that my behavior was placing their offspring's lungs in danger? Were they formulating even more obscene accusations? A hundred times, in the press, I had observed the ease children have in accusing adults of the worst crimes, without any possibility of denial.

As I went to the police station on the following Tuesday, I had made up my mind to tell everything exactly as it happened, without any evasion. The guard on duty began by examining my ID cards and then had me go through the metal detector before he pointed to the elevator and sent me through a labyrinth of hallways to the Juvenile Division.

There, a curt secretary asked me to wait in a room with yellowish walls. A poster hanging on the wall showed toddlers running about; behind them the threatening shadow of a man was outlined, beneath this caption: "Protect your children!" Refusing to give in to fear, I waited patiently for a good half-hour before the secretary asked me to follow her to the Chief Inspector's door.

The man was not unfriendly at first. Seated behind his desk, he had the sparse hair, the fine features, the elocution of a cultivated individual and—something that seemed to me like a mark of solidarity—he was smoking a cigarette. Almost ready to fraternize, I dared take a pack out of my pocket and asked him if I could.... He acquiesced, asking, in mocking tones:

"So is smoking your alibi?"

Why was he talking about alibis? I decided to smile and said, in an almost relaxed way:

"What do you mean, 'alibi'? Alibi for what?"

Cigarette in his mouth, the Chief Inspector fiddled with a pretty ivory paperweight. He glanced at me quickly and suddenly asked me, ironically:

"You like young adult literature? Disney movies?"

"Why should I be interested in such rubbish?"

"According to what I know, you aren't seen very often with children. You don't have any, is that right?"

He went from one question to another, following some strange logic. Whether or not I was interested in childhood, my behavior seemed to have something weird in it *in its essence.* This man, though, seemed intelligent, and I supposed he was testing me. Without waiting any longer, I decided to make things as clear as possible:

"Listen, Inspector, there's nothing secret about how I use my time. I live quietly with my companion, who can confirm this for you."

By insisting on my conjugal relations, which were banally heterosexual, I thought I was scoring a decisive point. He was silent for a bit, then went on:

"You haven't had any children with your companion?"

My mistake, this time, was to get impatient. His reproach seemed to convey Latifa's pressing questions. Why did they all want me to have children? In an exaggerated surge of exaspera-tion, and as if in order to bring an end to suspicion, I shouted:

"No, I don't have any children, because children get on my nerves, they're intrusive, they walk all over me. The municipal administration has been transformed into a daycare center. My colleagues—men with university degrees!—are like an army of nursery nannies. As for me, I don't look for children, I run away from them, is that clear?"

From the policeman's silence, I understood it was only too clear. He asked again, his voice suave:

"Why run away from them? Are you afraid of doing stupid things?"

The spirals of smoke that were rising up in his office still led me to believe that an understanding was possible:

"Frankly, I don't know what you're getting at! We might as well stop here, Inspector."

"*Chief* Inspector. You know, the problem with perverts is that they always deny everything, especially crimes against children. Most of the time, it's an intelligent man, your age, somewhat cultivated and seemingly normal...."

Crime against children. He had uttered the terrible phrase, that worst accusation of them all, the one that, more surely than any other, puts you in prison with harsh sentences. Two years earlier, under pressure of the victims' associations, the law had banished from the language the term "pedophile," which was deemed too complacent for criminals (there was, in this word, an idea of a "love of children" that was incompatible with the horror of the charges). Now the expression "crime against children" was preferred—which brought new confusions with it, since any person showing disagreeable behavior towards children risked being placed in the category of sexual perverts. Supposing that the Chief Inspector was a connoisseur of these nuances, I decided to dot the "i"'s:

"If I understand correctly, Chief Inspector, you suspect me of sexual perversion, of 'pedophilia,' as they used to say.

Except for that fact that, I repeat, I am a *pedophobe,* completely pedophobic!"

"To the point of doing them harm?"

"That's not what I mean. I don't even hate them! I don't see them, they don't interest me, I couldn't care less about them. To me, they are human larvae, little animals devoid of all interest."

"And with animals, you can do anything you like, without any scruples, isn't that right? Like enticing a little girl into the fourth-floor bathroom in Administration City and exhibiting yourself in front of her...."

For the first time, his face expressed fury. Terrified, I tried to sound as sincere as possible:

"Chief Inspector, sir, she came in by surprise. I was just in the process of smoking my cigarette."

I added in hushed tones, to awaken the smoker's solidarity:

"Can you believe that it's the only place in the building where the alarm won't go off?"

"And so why wasn't the door locked properly? And why were your pants down?"

The Chief Inspector knew every detail of the scene. It was as if the affair had taken on weight and mass in ten days; as if it had been transformed into a "case" full of mystery, lies and horror. Once again, I felt as if I were a child again, dispossessed of all adult dignity, forced to justify each detail:

"I must have forgotten to bolt it...."

"Forgotten, of course: let the little children come to me!"

I decided to let that go, and went on:

"The pants—how should I say it...every time I smoke a cigarette, I lower my pants...."

The policeman sniggered:

"That's interesting!"

"Yes, naturally, I lower my pants so people will think I'm really going to the bathroom, if anyone's waiting behind the door."

"And how would this person know that you had lowered your pants, since you were behind the door?"

"Really, Chief Inspector. You know very well that the rustle of clothes, the belt being unfastened, make a characteristic noise. From this noise, a person waiting outside the toilet stalls knows that the user is in the process of dressing himself again."

I caught my breath. What kind of sentence was I in the process of uttering? How could I spend all this time explaining to a policeman how I use the toilets at Administration City? In a new fit of impatience—as if we were people of good faith and as if I had the freedom to conclude things—I exclaimed:

"Listen, this is completely ridiculous, let's stop it there, please!"

"Frankly, I wouldn't advise you to take that tone. It's up to me to decide when we stop."

The Chief Inspector hesitated another instant. He bent over the pile of papers on his desk, silently reread a passage; then he straightened to summarize the situation in a perfectly relaxed and, once again, almost friendly tone:

"Me, I think you're guilty. I studied your file carefully: you are a cultivated man, a little solitary, inclined to be hostile to children—as if in fact you were afraid of something. Maybe you haven't actually done the deed yet, but you have the right profile to do the deed sooner or later...."

Whatever I said would just reinforce his preconceived theory. Could I try to change the way things stood? One last time, I dug deep into my remaining resources in order to demonstrate my innocence:

"And what about the boxer shorts, did she tell you about the boxer shorts?"

"What boxer shorts?"

"I'm telling you, Inspector, that my boxer shorts were up. Surely the little girl told you that! If I had wanted to commit indecent exposure, I would have pulled them down. Isn't that proof that I was there *to smoke a cigarette?*"

"Apparently you also had a screwdriver in your hand."

"Yes, a little screwdriver to unseal the window, so as to get rid of the smoke. You'll find it in my house, in the tool box."

"The problem is, the little girl claims you threatened her with this screwdriver!"

Once again I lost my cool.

"She said that, the little brat? Well, sir, it's not true. I chased her out of the bathroom so she wouldn't bother me while I was smoking, that's all!"

The policeman looked me right in my eyes:

"You know what, I've seen my share of guys like you, and most of them ended up confessing. But in your precise case, many questions come up. For the cigarette in the bathroom, your administration will deal with that directly with you. The cigarette butt out the window, that's more troublesome, there's the complaint from that woman for the risk you made her run; her lawyer is demanding damages and compensation."

He said this while checking his file, his finger on the notes piled up in front of him; then he swallowed a little saliva and went on:

"I hope for your sake that the judge will decide to let things rest there; but that will mean I've failed. Because, personally, I have no intention whatsoever of letting you go."

He had uttered these last words almost kindly, and pushed his amiability to the point of describing the procedure:

"In fact, everything will depend on the little girl. I interviewed her the day before yesterday, but she didn't finish her explanations. We will consult her again next week, along with psychologists, and I hope she will tell us what actually happened."

I was stunned by so much bad faith. He wanted at all cost to discover something vile, for a reason that he himself pointed out:

"You know, in my profession, there is one absolute rule: Children never lie. I could decide to be subtle, to take into account your thousands of good reasons for being innocent. But first and foremost I have to go back to that golden rule: to listen to the little girl so as not to risk—out of imprudence—putting other children in danger. If there were only one chance in a hundred that you're guilty, I'd support putting you in custody, on remand.... But that's up to the judge to decide."

Had he uttered the word "custody"? Had I already fallen that low? Cynical till the end of the interview, the Chief Inspector got up to accompany me and took me fraternally by my shoulder, saying:

"For now, you remain at liberty. But you should expect another summons."

I left the office reeling. Outside the police station, my first reflex was to go through the iron gate of nearby Queen's Park and sit down on a bench, near the duck pond. I've always liked watching ducks gliding over the water, in this artificial setting of shrubbery and rocks submerged like cliffs; I like seeing them setting their webbed feet on the artificial island they're the kings of, then shaking themselves off and waddling in a line, one behind the other. After I sat down, I remained motionless in blissfully happy contemplation, as if I just needed to breathe, calmly, as I repeated to myself: "I don't want them to keep me from seeing the ducks. I don't want to go to prison."

I started walking again like an automaton. Instead of going straight home, I went into a café, where I ordered a beer. I would have told all my misfortunes to the bartender... except that it was a question of a *crime against children,* the type of crime you don't talk about. In any case, the waiter and the customers, along with the entire country at this instant, had their eyes riveted on the TV to follow the latest news about Désiré Johnson—the real-life courtroom soap opera that would reach its climax, this afternoon, with live coverage of the last cigarette.

6

"Television viewers everywhere, we are gathered here together to share an extraordinary moment of emotion and to learn the outcome of this affair that has been the talk of the town for over two weeks. You only had to turn on your TVs to be informed, questioned, touched, and to take part yourselves in the debate. The live report you will watch in a few moments on the Justice Channel is itself controversial, despite the assent of the legal authorities. Some people have publicly voiced the opinion that this event should have taken place behind closed doors. That is not our opinion, and we congratulate ourselves on the transparency of this finale, which marks a threefold victory: a victory for the Law, whose sentence will finally be carried out; a victory for the prisoner condemned to death, Désiré Johnson, who, in a few minutes, will light his last cigarette, *live;* finally, victory for his sponsor, the General Tobacco Company, which provided the technical means by which this last wish can be carried out: a program that is being watched throughout the entire world by tens of millions of television viewers...."

Despite the energetic tone of the statement, the announcer's voice has an overtone of gravity. Holding his microphone as he stands in front of the camera, his hair gently fluttering in the wind, he isn't forgetting that he is presenting the end of a man's life, a man who murdered a police officer. For two weeks, discussions about Johnson, capital punishment, and the right to smoke have divided political parties, groups of friends, families. In some bars, customers have come to blows as a way of expressing their viewpoints. Before he went on the air, the announcer had sought the correct attitude that would suit the conclusion of this legal imbroglio: he ended up adopting this mixture of enthusiasm and sober emotion. The time for expert discussion is over; now it's a matter of experiencing an emotional moment, with the help of the General Tobacco Company. The red-and-gold logo of the multinational adorns little flags put up around the wall where, in a moment, the condemned man will savor his final pleasure, before he goes back inside the prison to receive the lethal injection.

"As you know, viewers at home, after the decision of the Supreme Court of Justice rejecting the appeal of the lawyer Maren Pataki (who had requested a delay of the execution), but recognizing the condemned man's unrescinable right to carry out his last wish, the administration of the penitentiary was confronted with a novel situation. How can one smoke a cigarette in premises that are fully equipped with smoke detectors? How can one avoid the avalanche of litigations threatened by the anti-smoking leagues that were already laying siege to the establishment in order to demand the regulations be rigorously applied? How could the prison guards' union be appeased, along with an association of prisoners who were making it into a matter of principle: 'No passive smoking in our prison!'? On the other side, several delegates from personnel wanted to take advantage of the circumstances and agitate for the right to open a smoking room. That's when the General Tobacco Company let it be known that it was ready to provide all the means necessary to allow Désiré Johnson to smoke his cigarette while respecting the norms of security, without putting a strain on the prison administration's budget. After studying several hypotheses, the management and the legal authorities opted for this well-ventilated piece of land, situated a mile away from the detention center...."

The announcer's arm points out the little meadow strewn with spring flowers stretching out behind him. During the previous days, a six-foot-high fence was built around the field. Four sentry-boxes, one at each corner of the field, are occupied by heavily armed guards. The camera zooms in on several close-ups of their faces, protected by gas masks.

"...The men chosen to ensure control of this operation have received special equipment, designed to protect them from the emanations of tobacco. They will also, thanks to the General Tobacco Company, receive a special bonus for this activity outside the penitentiary center.... But let's take a look now at the table and chair placed at Désiré Johnson's disposal, so he can smoke his cigarette in complete calm...."

The camera pans slowly from the fence to the interior of the meadow strewn with dandelions, daisies, and violets. In the middle of this improvised garden a table and a garden chair are placed, both in white plastic made to look like wrought-iron.... The camera zooms in again to show the objects placed on the table by the organizers: an ashtray, a lighter, and a pack of cigarettes that, in keeping with current standards, bears the photo of a cancerous lung. The General Tobacco Company wanted to provide the condemned man with a special pack, without any morbid allusions. On this point, however, the anti-smoking associations won out: no favoritism for the criminal Désiré Johnson.

"But now there's some movement over at the prison.... Hello, Jack, can you hear me?"

The camera continues to pan over the flowering meadow, while a dialogue takes place in voice-over.

"Yes, Misha, I hear you fine. I am at the entrance to the prison, where the doors have just opened. We're waiting for the appearance, any minute now, of the van that will transport the condemned man to the place of execution.... I mean, the execution of his last wish!"

"It's interesting to note, isn't it, Jack, that the distance between the prison and this meadow fitted out by the General Tobacco Company is about a mile."

"One mile and 984 feet exactly. But here it is, Misha, the vehicle is leaving the prison!"

The image of the meadow fades, giving way to a long shot of the prison. We see a van emerging, escorted by two light armored cars, in case this affair of state inspires a terrorist group. The vehicles disappear down the road, then are quickly "recaptured" by the cameras positioned at the entrance to the field. The van slows down, then stops in front of the fence. Misha supplies a few more explanations:

"Among the debates aroused by what is now being called the Johnson Affair, one of the more delicate arguments concerns the right to broadcast publicly these final instants of a man's life. We should point out that the condemned man, questioned by his lawyer, Ms. Maren Pataki, gave his consent.... The prison administration could still have opposed this media coverage. On their side, the anti-smoking associations regret that a court decision could serve as a pretext for an advertising display in favor of cigarettes—advertising that is, by the way, banned...."

Some armed men have jumped out of the light-armored cars to take their places around the van, which is still closed.

"It seems, in fact, that the legal arguments have been settled in favor of the General Tobacco Company—certain lawyers affirm that the prison administration cannot legally carry out a smoking execution, unless it entrusts the organization of the execution to a subcontractor. In exchange for its support, the cigarette company wanted to obtain audiovisual rights to the event; but it had to agree not to do anything, during the broadcast, that could be perceived as disguised advertising for its cigarette brands. The president of the General Tobacco Company prefers to speak of a 'moment of reflection' in which he invites television viewers to participate, while respecting their opinions. But now, Jack, a guard is approaching to unlock the van. We are about to see the condemned man *live*, the incredible Désiré Johnson...."

As he utters this last sentence, Misha has raised his voice as if the show were beginning. Johnson gets out of the van in his prison uniform—a kind of orange canvas cut in one single piece. All the TV viewers fix their gaze on his wide shoulders, his Rasta dreads, his large green eyes.... An expression of satisfaction appears on his confident face, which seems to be looking for the camera, and coming to rest in front of it. Johnson no longer looks like a dumbfounded prisoner; he poses for his audience and puts both heavily-chained hands together, in a gesture of victory. The satisfaction of having obtained *what he wanted* seems to win out over the apprehension of the capital punishment that will be applied to him in less than an hour.

"We would have liked to interview the condemned man to gather his final impressions, to find out his opinion on the organization of the event, on the choice of this field.... The legal authorities, unfortunately, forbade us to approach Désiré Johnson, for understandable reasons. For this man is no saint. He has been found guilty of the murder of a police officer, a father of three children. The victim was forty-three years old. Today, the time has come for Johnson to pay his debt...."

Two guards guide the condemned man to the entrance of the smoking field. A third man comes forward to undo the handcuffs. Johnson, unchained, shakes his arms for a minute; he raises his head with a strange smile, then advances alone inside the fence, while the announcer continues:

"A strange murderer, who has always denied his crime, but who could not prevent himself from repeating during his trial: 'Frankly, if I had to kill someone, I'd have chosen a bastard like him!' It is understandable why the Court upheld the death penalty which is, remember, officially abolished throughout the Union, except in certain states and in certain cases, as for instance the murder of a member of the forces of order.... So it is without pity, but with a certain emotion, that we see Désiré Johnson move towards the garden table where his cigarette awaits him. A pretty amazing sight, isn't it, Jack?"

"Yes, when you think that this strange provocateur is living his final fifteen minutes in front of us! Especially when you think that he's living these final minutes with the suicidal thoughtlessness of a smoker!"

"You're right, Jack, that's the terrible paradox of this affair. You can understand why a man who will die wants to have a last smoke, but the interest aroused by his case shouldn't bring about a renewed approval of smoking!"

"Personally, I'm happy I stopped smoking seven years ago. But what fascinates us today is this legal first; this man being formally authorized to carry out his final wish, this man who is now being granted the object of his request."

During this exchange, the prisoner has made a few steps onto the grass, his face becoming increasingly radiant. There have been a number of still shots of him, first from one angle, then from another, taken by the cameras placed around the meadow. Now he bends down and kneels on the ground. He stretches out his hand and, with his index finger, strokes the petals of a daisy before delicately picking it. He then puts out his other hand, picks a violet, and begins to put together a bouquet. The announcers remain silent for several seconds, punctuated by brief exclamations:

"Incredible! What is he doing?"

"It looks like he's looking for something...."

"No, I think he's picking flowers!"

Misha's head reappears on the screen. He holds his microphone firmly, standing in front of the meadow where Johnson is still busy, kneeling down on the ground. Stunned, the announcer abandons the rigorous neutrality of his commentary:

"You are seeing this fantastic sight at the same time as I am. How can a man condemned to death for the murder of a police-man, on the verge of his own death, pause to pick wildflowers? I wish we could understand the meaning of this gesture."

"In any case, Misha, the people who thought of Johnson as a monster must be disappointed...."

"It looks like he's getting up now and approaching the table. Look: he's holding his bouquet of flowers in his hand...."

"Is that a final allusion to this earth that he is about to leave? I suppose he's going to light the cigarette now."

"What a strange juxtaposition! The cigarette, with its toxic tar; the wildflowers, symbol of freshness.... I imagine that more than one viewer must be wondering about Johnson's behavior."

The condemned man is standing next to the table. He does not sit down; on the contrary, he pushes the pack of cigarettes over to the edge, then he throws his daisies, dandelions, and violets in disarray over the surface of the white plastic. We see him shake himself again, in his plastic-covered orange uni-form. Suddenly, the image fades out; another camera takes over, showing the face of a guard under his anti-smoking mask, while Misha says, in a voice-over:

"It's incredible, Jack, something incredible is happening...."

"Tell us, Misha! We can't see what's happening. I think our producer is a little at a loss."

"He certainly is, since I think the condemned man Désiré Johnson is in the process of conveying a message."

"A message?"

The image returns to Johnson, bent over the table. We can just see his back, but Misha, thanks to the control-room screens, precisely describes the prisoner's gestures:

"I think he's drawing letters with the help of the wildflowers; as if he were trying to say something...."

"That would be a great scoop, Misha. You know that Johnson doesn't have the right to say anything on the occasion of this final wish! If he does so, that might even disturb the course of the broadcast."

"That's true, it's a risky bet; that's why our producer had an instant of hesitation. But it seems that the court is permitting us to go on, for now. I imagine Johnson wants to take advantage of the occasion to claim his innocence.... He is taking another daisy, and the words are beginning to be legible. I'll try to make them out.... Yes, that's it, it's...incredible!"

Johnson's large body finally stands up. His relaxed face turns towards the camera; then he moves aside and lets appear, in vegetable letters placed on the white table, this brief phrase made up of stems, petals, stamens; three words offered to millions of television viewers:

LONG LIVE LIFE

After a brief moment of silence, Misha's voice continues:

"You are discovering this phrase at the same time as we are. Incredible Johnson! One more time, he disconcerts everyone by not saying, 'I am innocent....' No, the meaning is much more general."

"That's true, Misha. A homage to life, written with flowers; it's hard to believe that such a phrase is coming from the brain of a murderer."

"If only this man, whom we'd like to think was innocent, had not repeated, during his trial, that he could easily have killed that police officer!"

"But remember that he also said, 'I could never harm an old person, a woman, or a child....'"

"A love of fragility that he has just expressed again. You know what's just come into my head, Jack?"

"No."

"Maybe this whole business with the cigarette was just a way to get to this point, an extraordinary strategy to make this message get through before he dies...."

As if to confirm these statements, Johnson finally sits down on the garden chair. He leans over to the table and grasps the pack, then takes out the prisoner's cigarette, brings it to his mouth and lights it. He has placed himself in such a way that the audience, while still seeing him smoke, can read the phrase written next to him, "Long live life."

"But why is this amazing man letting ambiguity hang over everything until the last second? Why, instead of shouting to save his skin, is he calling out to each person's conscience?"

Désiré Johnson is now savoring each puff of smoke, and he looks as if he were communing with the entire nation. Millions of television viewers interpret the message in their own way. Having gathered in their conference room on President Bush Avenue, the heads of the General Tobacco Company are thinking that with the participation of such an individual, their failing enterprise could easily make a comeback. The lawyer Maren Pataki, who failed in her attempts to obtain a pardon, understands that with such a client, all hopes are possible. The President of the Republic himself is overwhelmed by what he sees on his television set. He is thinking about the meaning of life and the emotional scandal the execution of such a man would produce. That at least is what one might imagine, while Johnson returns to the police van to be taken back to the prison and undergo the lethal injection. For the instant the vehicle enters the enclosure of the penitentiary center, the overexcited figure of Misha appears again on the screen, microphone in hand, to announce, a little breathlessly:

"Today, without a doubt, there will be one breaking news item after another. We have just learned that the President has telephoned at the last possible minute to grant his exceptional pardon to the condemned man Désiré Johnson."

7

After I'd reached Hydrangea Lane, I could still hear the Chief
Inspector's words: "I think you are guilty and, personally, I
have no intention whatsoever of letting you go..." All along
the sidewalk, the flower gardens smelled sweetly of spring, but
his horrible threat made this beauty seem fragile, and made me
want to burst out crying. Bounding out from the house, Sarko
ran up to greet me, and I pressed him against my leg in despair.
Crushed by the accusation, I wondered how I could tell Latifa
about the scene that had just taken place. From my pale com-
plexion and my stammers, she understood right away. She
insisted tactfully enough that I describe the interview and the
policeman's conclusion exactly as it happened. In the silence
that followed, my companion looked at me with that confidence that I knew so well in her, that energy of civilized beings

who are convinced that a solution can always be found, and she asserted:

"We'll fight!"

She was tall, healthy, smiling, and her combativeness, this time, cheered me up. Didn't Latifa's very personality, her radiant beauty, constitute demonstration enough of my innocence? How could the lover of such a goddess be hiding the personality of a pervert? Unquestionably, her personality played in my favor. Fighting the anguish that was knotting my stomach, I decided to follow her example—the first thing to do was to find a lawyer.

She probably thought she was doing me good in mentioning, in the course of the dinner, the name of Maren Pataki, who had become famous after having saved Désiré Johnson from death. The connection made between two such disproportionate causes could seem alarming, but Latifa was aiming high; she wanted the best there was, no matter the price. Quite naturally, her attention had settled on the woman who, under the eyes of the media, had just allowed the black criminal to escape lethal injection. Not knowing all the details, I was unaware that Ms. Pataki had played no part in Johnson's rescue, and that she had on the contrary precipitated his condemnation by her clumsy pleading for the defense. Johnson all by himself had the idea for the last cigarette. Johnson alone had saved his skin by his incredible televised performance. I would discover all that much later on, but, for now, Latifa had another vision of the affair: By saving this man thanks to the "condemned man's cigarette," Maren Pataki had become the champion of smoking-rights defenders. If she had been able to get a condemned murderer pardoned, she would have no difficulty in proving innocent a simple smoker wrongly suspected of a crime against children. What's more, she benefited from the support of the powerful General Tobacco Company that might see, in my case, an additional opportunity to incite smokers to stand up for their rights.

The first difficulty was making contact with this woman at the height of her glory, transformed into the official manager of "Désiré" (as everyone now called him), the friend of life, children, and flowers. Latifa moved heaven and earth to contact her, and persuade the lawyer that we weren't nuisances lured by her notoriety, demonstrate that my affair was interesting, and that she also had means to pay for her services. We didn't know that the General Tobacco Company, faced with the sudden amplitude of the Johnson Affair, had just appointed a major law firm to replace the court-appointed lawyer and obtain a retrial. Maren Pataki's final hope rested on the unpredictable whims of Johnson, who could decide to get in the way. In the meantime, taking advantage of her temporary fame, she hurried to respond favorably to all the solicitations addressed to her; Latifa's call seemed to her one opportunity among others to enlarge her clientele.

Every morning, Désiré made the front page in the papers. The presidential pardon had been followed by the appearance of a petition, signed by the greatest figures in the country, in favor of a new investigation: "We find it hard to believe that this friend of life, children, and flowers is a murderer. Isn't his only crime being poor and having black skin?"

For some days, the idea of sharing a lawyer with such a popular man raised my morale. Moreover, during our first interview in her tiny office, Ms. Pataki showed a solid confidence about my fate: nothing serious could happen, since there was no hard proof. However, I didn't like the way she interrupted my urgent questions with a maternal smile:

"Don't get upset, there's no use in getting agitated!"

Turning to Latifa, she added, in a tone of feminine complicity:

"I feel as if I'm seeing my twelve-year-old son. Always impatient, always anxious to find out the answer!"

The smiles they had exchanged came back to my mind like an unpleasant noise.

At Administration City, I had asked for a special leave of absence to prepare my defense. Every morning, I walked down the garden path to empty the mailbox where I dreaded finding the summons of the examining magistrate, which arrived one week later. In that day's paper there was a new photo of Désiré, his bouquet in hand. With a certain dizziness, I thought that this man had just escaped death thanks to a cigarette, whereas I...I shivered, imagining where the mirror symmetry of our situations might lead.

Latifa, who is not officially my wife, did not have the right to accompany me to the hearing. I left her in the vast lobby of the court house. She hugged me, then tried to reassure me again:

"Stay calm. Just say what happened and everything will be fine. But above all, have confidence in your lawyer."

On this last point, she was wrong—since it's difficult to have confidence in an absent lawyer. Ms. Pataki had not yet arrived when I entered the office of the examining magistrate, a fat woman with a schoolboy haircut who welcomed me with a thundering:

"Sit down, Mr. Lover-of-Little-Girls!"

As with the Chief Inspector, the die seemed to have been already cast. My denials would serve no purpose, and again I was filled with fear. To try to escape her ogress stare, I looked fixedly at a large oil painting hanging behind her, over the desk: a painting done in the old-fashioned, pompous style representing a group of naked children, half-angels half-babies, frolicking in a puffy cloud. The painter had reproduced, with infinite attention to detail, the chubby shapes, the color of the buttocks, the little pink breasts. Before I could open my mouth, the judge thundered—as if she had just caught me in a trap:

"Aren't they pretty, my little girls? But watch out, no touching!"

The sudden arrival of Ms. Pataki didn't make a better impression. Full to the brim of her recent notoriety, the little disheveled woman entered the office carrying a large pile of files, triumphantly explaining that she was keeping the Johnson file, at the condemned man's request. She barely excused herself for her lateness, which earned her a nasty remark from the magistrate. Far from letting herself be intimidated, my lawyer reeled off her argument, which rested on three points:

1) The suppression of smoking zones in the administration buildings was deplorable; this new affair emphasized this. My mad spell in the bathroom was certainly linked to frustration. A large cigarette company was studying the possibility of reestablishing—at its own expense—smoking rooms in the administration buildings.

Her reference to the General Tobacco Company seemed premature to me. But why, especially, was she talking about a "mad spell"? The demonstration bore upon two other points:

2) There was no question of calling the word of a child into question. My legal record showed no precedent, in any case,

and a confrontation with the victim seemed indispensable to establish the facts rigorously.

3) Impossible to judge such an affair without also taking into account situations of incest or indecent exposure to which I might have been subjected during my childhood. Therefore, she requested a psychiatric evaluation.

I was speechless. Then I turned to her, stammering:

"But that's not it at all! Nothing happened in the bathroom!"

Seeing the disarmed look of my lawyer, I discovered that my situation was more delicate than I had thought. Even for the person in charge of defending me, it seemed difficult to cast doubt on the statements of this little girl. That's why Ms. Pataki had opted for a subtle advance, which included a partial acceptance of my guilt. She added, in a tone that was meant to be reassuring:

"Trust me!"

The examining magistrate still wore her man-eating smile:

"As your lawyer has rightly recalled, there is no question of doubting the word of a child. In response to your request, however, I have summoned the victim, who is in the next room, so that she can confirm her serious accusations."

She swallowed her saliva and looked at me more severely:

"I am going to have little Amandine come in now, but let me make this very clear: you do not have the right to address her, except at my request. After the trauma she has undergone, your presence will be hard enough to bear."

What could I have said after that? My point of view was of interest to no one, and my word had no importance whatsoever. Mechanically, I raised my exasperated gaze to the chubby babies hanging over the judge, who repeated, snickering:

"No touching!"

The little girl entered the office. Scarcely did I have time to recognize her than her mother—an aging Lolita in a black faux-leather skirt and a purple jacket—said to me in disgusted tones:

"Scumbag! Guys like you should be tortured for what they do to kids!"

The judge let her reel off these insane remarks along with other threats. When she had finished, I thought it fitting to point out:

"I never touched your daughter, ma'am."

"I asked you to be quiet, sir," the examining magistrate cut in curtly. "Tell me, my little one, Amandine, that is your name, isn't it?"

The little girl nodded her head without looking at me. Her face was bent down towards the floor and the entire interrogation took place like this, without her raising her eyes towards me.

"Do you recognize this gentleman, Amandine?"

She didn't answer. I looked at the ogress sitting behind her desk. Two big jowls fell from her vein-filled face that, suddenly, resolved itself into a tender grimace:

"My little Amandine, I know that it's very hard for you, to think about what happened. So I am going to tell you myself, and you'll tell me if it's true, okay?"

"Okay."

"Did this gentleman lower his pants?"

"Yes, ma'am!"

"Did he leave the door open?"

"Yes, ma'am!"

"Did he make you afraid?"

"Yes, he shouted at me. He had a screwdriver!"

"Did he touch you?"

The little girl still looked at the floor. Hesitating for an instant, she raised her glasses up to her mother, who put her hand on her shoulder and patted her little head:

"Go on, darling, you can tell her."

"Yes, ma'am, he touched me."

"I know this is very difficult, Amandine, but can you tell me where he touched you?"

Amandine again questioned her mother, who was visibly becoming impatient and was suddenly more authoritarian:

"Go on, tell her!"

"Yes, ma'am, between my legs."

At these words, while Lolita squeezed her child harder, I exploded and turned to the woman I had taken to be my lawyer:

"I can't let things like that be said..."

"I asked you to be quiet," the judge cut in. "I know it's difficult for you to respect a child, but shut your mouth now! Thank you, ma'am, and you too my little Amandine. I promise you that this gentleman won't hurt you anymore."

Almost nothing else happened. After Amandine and her mother left, the examining magistrate assured my lawyer that, given this distressing testimony, it seemed indispensable to place me in temporary detention and to carry out a search of my home. She added that an investigation was underway of all the children who used the second-floor hallway at Administration City. In her deposition, Amandine's mother had implied that others could have been the victims of my fondling, as certain nightmares of her daughter's led her to believe. Maren Pataki found nothing to reply. Guards entered to handcuff me and take me to the station. Seeing my life suddenly collapse into this grotesque catastrophe, I began to fight, while the lawyer contented herself with repeating:

"Trust me. For now, I'll plead indecent exposure without fondling or violence. You might have to accept medical treatment, but we'll fight and you'll get out."

"Tell Latifa I need her!"

I had almost shouted this phrase. My fists shackled in two circles of cold metal, I was already entering my captive condition. Placed in custody at the St. Lawrence Prison, I learned a few days later the cute nickname of "Sudden Death" that Ms. Pataki was given in the world of jailbirds.

*

Only the instinct for survival prevented me from losing my grip. My situation, looked at objectively, was terrifying: to go instantaneously from the status of executive, of a well-off Western intellectual, an adult man free in his movements, to the condition of a prisoner incarcerated by the law; to be suddenly deprived of my basic rights, subjected to a routine and to a set of regulations, taken away from the light of day, threatened with abuse by my co-detainees; to see myself potentially ruined financially from paying the lawyers and victims' compensation.... Some people would lose their reason, would let themselves die. Especially when, even within the class of outlaws, you're classified as belonging to the most abject category, from the simple fact that your case file mentions the worst possible misdeed: *crime against children*. In such a case, you will benefit from no form of compassion or solidarity.

From overhearing idle talk, I had thought for a long time that I preferred criminals to policemen, prisoners to judges. My spontaneous sympathy carried me outside the laws of this cruel society.... I had to end up here to understand that prisoners are just as abject as humanity as a whole; that, inside prisons, they establish the same pitiless social hierarchy; that their lower morality reproduces current morality, in a simpler and more brutal version. They adopt all the trashy media items dictated by the fantasies of the day. As if to make up for their own past crimes, they avenge themselves with redoubled fury on those whom society considers the lowest of all.

As soon as I entered this trap, I scarcely had any time to feel sorry for myself; all my energy was taken up by another urgency: to escape their criminal's righteousness by avoiding saying why I was there—which isn't easy, in a place where you display your crime the way you present your resumé on the outside.... Anticipating my hesitation, the guards had taken it upon themselves to inform everyone; at least I suppose so, since, as soon as I took my first walk in the prison courtyard, I found myself all alone on the edge, while half a dozen detainees were huddled together, glancing at me anxiously. At the whistle-blow, they scattered, but, soon, they passed by close to me, one after the other, whispering their compliments into my ear, graced with a little sign of their fingers across their throat, slicing like a steel blade.

"We'll do you in, you chester, you filthy child molester!"

I should have answered that I myself had no particular sympathy for that category of the population. I should have reminded them that I was innocent and presumed so until my trial. But in prison, the presumption of innocence exists even less than it does elsewhere. So the litany of threats went on until the end of the exercise period, with an even more precise instruction:

"Better not go to sleep, if you ever want to wake up again!"

As I would learn later on, the individual who whispered these gentle words to me had killed his wife's lover by beating his head against the floor. Instead of looking to his improbable defense, he was devoting his energy to a new cause in the service of Justice: settling his score with an enemy of children. Scarcely did I have time to understand his threat when I received a quick jab in my kidneys, while another voice murmured:

"No pity for guys who rape kids!"

This one had found a guy carelessly leaning on his car in the parking-lot and beaten him with a baseball bat. The victim was finishing his existence in a wheelchair but the criminal, thanks to me, had just discovered a more promising horizon: he just had to purify this prison of some riffraff, of whom I represented the disgusting image, with my middle-class forty-something look, luring little girls into bathrooms. At the end of the exercise period, I walked fearfully, glancing nervously around me. I was locked up in a recess yard, in the midst of cruel kids who wouldn't give me any chance. The guards didn't bat an eyelid. Was it out of weariness, because it was impossible to intervene in such small matters? Or was there a secret complicity with the prisoners whose values they shared, in this hierarchy that relegated me to the lowest rung in the social ladder?

Back in my cell, I leaned against the wall, my eyes moist. In vain I repeated that it was just a temporary detention and that the nightmare would soon be over; I was beginning to understand that they wouldn't give me any chance. Weeks would go by, months maybe, before the end of the investigation and the demonstration of my innocence. My only hope lay in Latifa's determination, who was using all her energy to get me out; but I didn't have the right to see her every day, and I had to bear up in these abominable conditions.... Obviously, I could have had it even worse, could have been locked up with a brute who tortured me. No doubt the people in charge of the prison preferred to avoid dangerous situations that risked complicating their lives; so they had me sharing this cell with another child criminal who, for his part, had confessed all his crimes.

While I was sniveling by the wall, Paolo, sitting on his bed, was leafing through a news magazine in which there was half a column about the apotheosis of his social career. He was also in his forties, his skull already bald, his vacant eyes behind glasses with one lens broken by a detainee. He expressed himself in a timid voice and remained by himself most of the time (the last time he had gone out to the exercise yard, he had returned with a broken tooth). From the age of fifteen, Paolo had experienced an irresistible attraction to little boys, to whom he loved showing his private parts. Perhaps, in some long-ago village, this poor perversion might have been better tolerated.... The fact remains that, out of concern for prevention, after having been imprisoned a first time, Paolo had entered the endless cycle of medical treatments, paroles, psychiatric internments that still hadn't kept him from repeating his attempts.

Two months earlier, he had undressed himself in front of a little seven-and-a-half-year-old Vietnamese boy, then let him go after he'd made him swear not to say anything about it. Paolo had told me this story in detail, and I found it difficult to understand the excitation this infantile gaze at his genitals procured; I found pathetic the irresistible attraction he felt for these barely formed beings who had literally shattered his life. But, despite my compassion, I couldn't accept the fact that I was put in the same box as him, as if my guilt were acknowledged. This connection played into the hands of the other prisoners, who thought of us as a duo, and sometimes shouted at us in the hallway, resorting to the discourse of taunting feminization ("So, bitches, you like fucking each other?"), when they weren't making an appeal for popular justice ("Watch out, two child molesters are locked up in 145").

On the morning of the second day, I decided to go to the showers. Paolo refused to go there for fear of getting hit; he gave off a stale stench, despite his ablutions in the cell washbasin. As for me, I still had a sense of hygiene and a certain confidence in the role of the guards in charge of ensuring my protection. So I went my way, without imagining exactly what was in store for me. A little embarrassed when it came time to get undressed, I timidly advanced into the cloud of hot water, where the news already seemed to have been passed along. I immediately noticed the cruel looks, then various phrases flung out like spit, while I approached the group: "It's the molester. He makes me want to puke...."

The insults raised a barrier of shame between us, and soon I found myself alone, at the end of the shower room, beneath one of the showerheads that rained down on me while the other prisoners washed themselves at a distance. The guard put his head in from time to time. All of a sudden, in the patter of water on the tiles, I could make out a new series of tirades, quieter, obviously aimed at me:

"He has a nice ass, the new one."

"Almost like a child's ass."

"Not surprising, considering his tastes!"

My heart beat faster. I tried to seem indifferent and keep soaping myself, but they were all looking at me now. Their tone had something brutal and excited about it.

"Turn around a little, molester, so I can see your little hole!"

"That way, honey, I want to see your ass too...."

Completely terrified, I was fixed in place. To reach the exit, I would have to go in front of them and, now, the guard had disappeared. One hand between their legs, the detainees uttered their threats in an undertone, so as not to trigger the alarm:

"You want us to do to you what you do to little girls?"

At that critical instant, a powerful voice rose up and drowned out the others with the force of a thunderclap:

"Let the guy alone. The next one who bothers him will have to deal with me!"

Who was daring to speak like that? What god was coming to my aid? The guard hadn't returned but, from the back of the shower room, a human shape had started moving in my direction, while the others backed off to give him room.... Or rather a human animal: 330 pounds of flesh and fat, his body covered in hair and soap bubbles, the man slowly advanced through the burning-hot steam. A few heads had turned round, full of incomprehension:

"But, Lulu! It's a crime against children!"

"What do you know about it? Touch one single hair on his head and I'll take care of you!"

Sometimes, in life, at the most desperate moment of solitude, a gesture of solidarity materializes, an attitude that breaks through the surrounding cowardliness, before which the rats end up fleeing. At that instant, the horde that was encircling me broke up; each person lowered his head and went back to washing himself, while the enormous mass of this mountain of flesh advanced, his face round as a Buddha's, with a sumo-wrestler's arms, his legs slightly bow-legged on the tiles. The matted hair on his skin, which glistened with soap, formed a dense vegetation over his whole body, and a minuscule sex emerged in the midst of this forest. With the calm of a righter of wrongs, he shifted the weight of his body from one leg to the other. The detainees kept their heads bowed without daring to say anything. When he was quite close to me, I fixed my gaze on this unexpected protector, with a mixture of gratitude and confidence. Just then his big child's face broke out smiling; then Lulu unfolded his enormous arm, put forward his hairy, pudgy hand, and placed it on my hip, declaring to the others:

"He's my pal, and I advise you not to get on his nerves."

For someone in my situation, to be able to count on a strong personality, unquestioned in the community, constitutes a guarantee of physical and mental soundness. You can find the same law in most political or administrative careers that require you to meet the right protector at the right moment.... Except that here, unlike politics or administration, not to find the right protector would have exposed me to truly painful consequences. Without the intervention of Lulu, I would have lost a good portion of teeth, then adopted that behavior of submission and withdrawal into the self that's symptomatic of abused individuals. Lulu spared me all that. From our first encounter in the shower, he looked at me as a decent, vulnerable individual. Despite his heaviness and his rough language, he shows a kind of gentleness towards me, and I have become his confidant. At every exercise period, he waits for me to join him, apart from the others. Sitting on the steps, he tells me about his exploits, how he was a bouncer at nightclubs before he killed a "Chink" (he doesn't like the yellow races). He tells me all this as if it's a fairytale; from time to time, a phrase sheds light on his friendship for me:

"Now, even intelligent and respectable White people like you are put in prison. That's something I can't accept...."

He sometimes embellishes his analysis with an additional explanation:

"Everything that's happening to you is the fault of whores; we should never have let whores have all the power."

Thinking of Amandine's mother, I have to agree that Lulu isn't completely wrong. As to the rest, my moral sense rebels at hearing these racist, sexist inanities uttered without being able to react. But I don't have any choice. Lulu is strong, Lulu strikes fear in everyone. Even when he isn't next to me, the others now content themselves with a mocking smile whose meaning I know very well since, for them, I have become *Lulu's wife*. It's in these precarious social, material, and psychological conditions that I wait, day after day, for news from my lawyer and especially from Latifa who, outside, is continuing to do everything she can to save me.

8

The Vice President in charge of Public Relations appeared in person under the awning and walked toward the limousine door. Although prepared for this meeting, he was struck by the extraordinary collectedness of his guest, this nonchalance of a man who had been condemned to death holding out his hand and smiling. Looking up at the General Tobacco Company skyscraper, the tall black man remarked, shaking his head:

"Pretty cool!"

Désiré had swapped his orange prisoner's uniform for a Gucci jogging suit and an air-soled pair of Nikes. The gold chain around his neck might be a reminder that he was a former criminal but, aside from this one detail, his whole behavior seemed calm and detached. He shook his head slowly as he smiled, without saying a word; and the Vice President thought with admiration that this ingenuousness was hiding a first-rate

intellectual and strategic mind, as the business with the cigarette had proven. That is how the media were analyzing the
behavior of the former condemned man, who in a few weeks
had become one of the most popular men in the country, the
leader of the fight against capital punishment, for smokers'
rights, for children, and for flowers; in short, a champion of life
and the various causes he had embodied as he was carrying out
his last wish. Although still accused until the retrial, no one
wanted to view this man as a murderer anymore. The Vice
President himself was thinking more and more firmly that it
would be in his company's interest to provide financial support
to the counter-investigation and the legal counterattack.

He was disappointed to see Ms. Pataki emerge from the
other door. Her face tired and pale, the lawyer walked around
the vehicle and came up to stand next to her client like a body-
guard. Ever since Désiré Johnson's conditional release, she
never let him take a step on his own. It was less a matter, for
the young woman, of preparing the criminal counteroffensive
than of keeping under her thumb a defendant who represented
almost all of her income. So as not to be outmaneuvered by the
General Tobacco Company, she had to keep up a special rela-
tionship with her client. Everyone had to understand that it
was useless to address Désiré without first going through her.
For that, she took advantage of the Rasta's laxness, who never
forced anything, and contented himself with a few symbolic
gestures—like that "V" for victory he showed to the TV cam-

eras gathered around him. Seeing this woman always shadow-ing him (she practically slept in the sitting room of his hotel, a suite at the Four Seasons paid for by the General Tobacco Company), Désiré had ended up accepting this presence as a natural one...except for that fact that the lawyer Maren Pataki saw her role slipping little by little down to that of press attaché, private secretary, housekeeper, and a whole slew of other professions that she willingly accepted, so as not to lose her goose with the golden eggs.

While the elevator rose to the fourteenth floor, Désiré looked at the Vice President with a large smile, then repeated:

"Your place is pretty cool!"

"Thank you, I think we are...quite happy here, in fact. This building was constructed in 1927."

"You know where I can find a little grass?"

Surprised, the executive grinned and stammered:

"I'm sorry, but I don't think that's part of our diversifi-cation yet...."

Johnson scrutinized him with that imperturbable smile that would have seemed imbecilic if it weren't hiding a genius that was recognized by everyone today. Maren took on the amused look of a woman who is familiar with psycholog-ical terms:

"Never mind him—he's like a little boy. He reminds me of my son who's just turned twelve. You think he's trying to pro-voke you, but he's just having fun!"

They entered the conference room where Maren had been received the first time. Walking over to the windows, Désiré looked briefly at the city beneath his feet; then they sat down in the lounge area and began to talk about this new life, and the upcoming trial. The Vice President cleared his throat before starting out:

"We have just been putting the final touches on a media plan to tell about how you got out of prison. You will be on all the major TV news shows. Perhaps you should meet our press attachés...."

Before Désiré could reply, Maren Pataki indicated the process that had to be followed:

"Give me the schedule in detail, I'll take care of everything."

The director looked at Johnson questioningly. The defendant confirmed with a blissful smile:

"That's fine, she'll take care of it."

Searching in his pocket, the former condemned man took out a pack of cigarettes. He was preparing to light one of them when his gaze met the executive's, who timidly explained to him:

"I'm sorry, but this is a non-smoking area."

As he uttered these words, he was only repeating the regulations. All of a sudden, he interrupted himself, annoyed: he had just repeated the scene of the failed execution, almost word for word! This remark could seem in very bad taste at a time when he was welcoming his guest. Far from seeming upset, Johnson looked astonished again:

"No smoking, in a place where they make cigarettes!"

"I'm sorry, sir, it's the labor law. In professional buildings, smoking is prohibited; our employees are just as vigilant on this point as other workers. And I must confess to you that, personally, I am...inconvenienced by tobacco" (he coughed as he uttered these words). "But we have reserved spaces: at the other end of the room, behind the glass door, if you like."

Always accommodating, Désiré Johnson went over to the smoking zone, gently shrugging his shoulders. The Vice President took advantage of his absence to sound out the lawyer:

"You don't think that...given this new trial, it might be good for you to have the support of a team of experts?"

Maren was expecting this question, as a prelude to her planned ousting. Still, she observed that her interlocutor was going about it gingerly, because of the influence she had over her client. She had to remain firm:

"Really, thank you for your solicitude; but Désiré is anxious for me to look after things on my own. So I'll continue to wage the battle, as I've already done with a certain success, isn't that right? And still with your financial support, I hope!"

The manager seemed perplexed:

"Still, you would have everything to gain...."

"I am an independent woman, I like investigating, I like the battlefield."

The man waved an understanding hand. Then his forehead wrinkled again, and he asked:

"Still, it must not be easy to take care of your other affairs, without a secretary, with such an important case as Désiré's? Your clientele risks suffering as a result."

Maren wanted to show that she was master of the situation:

"That's why I'm only accepting small, unimportant cases.... Which reminds me, did you get my e-mail about that poor guy accused of a crime against children after he smoked a cigarette in the bathroom at Administration City?"

"Frankly, that's not a case for us. Whatever he did, or didn't do, we keep our hands off crimes against children—it's too distasteful."

Désiré, who was returning from the smoking lounge, approved in a confident voice, like a man who knows the truth:

"Hands off children, you're right! Hands off life!"

The PR director turned around, smiling. He liked that last phrase. Here was the great Désiré, the one he had admired on TV, the one who had aroused a huge wave of popular support, the master-of-wisdom Désiré. Enthusiastic, the higher-up went on to the next subject:

"Tell me, dear... friend, aside from the media plan and the new trial, is there a fight, today, around which you'd like us to mobilize ourselves?"

Johnson had flopped into his chair with the slightly vulgar confidence of gangsters. He politely asked:

"Could I have a little drink? A whisky or something?"

"Of course, I'll call for one right away…"

As soon as the drink was ordered, the tall Rasta seemed to concentrate for an instant; then he turned a suddenly grave face to the PR director:

"Today, I see one single important fight; and frankly it isn't my own. It's the fight of the hostages in *A Martyr Idol*…."

"That's true!" his two interlocutors said approvingly.

The Vice President nodded his head, as if there were no possible discussion. Then he asked:

"But…you think you can do something for these unfortunate people?"

"I don't know, but what I do know is that we have to fight. What I do know is that May 5th marked a turning-point, and that we can't stand still with our arms crossed…"

"He's right," the lawyer hurried to repeat. "We can't ever think the same way after May 5th."

*

A thorough reading of the newspapers of that Wednesday, May 5th, might lead one to believe that it was a dreary day, one of those days when the world falls asleep, when the news idles to a stop. To keep the readers' attention, several headlines recalled on the first page the upcoming conditional release of Désiré Johnson, achieved by the efforts of his support committee; but already one felt as if the affair were becoming less important, as the threat of death became more remote. Rare were the readers who noticed, on the inside pages, this laconic communiqué distributed by a press agency; a few lines that would soon occupy the heart of the news—a few lines that, retrospectively, marked this Wednesday, May 5th, as one of the days when history wakes up and makes your blood run cold:

> The terrorist group "John Wayne's Conscience" has claimed responsibility for the kidnapping of six hostages in the Near East. Anxiety has grown for several days after the disappearance of civil and military aid workers on the road to Damascus. In a letter sent to the television network Allah No. 1, the group—which was unknown until today— threatened to proceed to execute the hostages, if it does not receive the payment of a ransom of 500 million dollars, to finance the development of "quality terrorism."

At first sight, the claim seemed like a farce; it was also sadly commonplace. For two years now, armed groups in the service of the vaguest causes were multiplying in the region; crooks had taken the place of religious groups to demand anything and everything. The affair seemed about to disappear after the governments concerned had declared there was no question of giving in to blackmail. It recovered all its magnitude, though, on the night of May 10th, when the Allah No. 1 Network broadcast another video tape on which six cowering hostages appeared, completely terrified. Around them, masked men brandished pistols and swords whose blades they held over the prisoners' necks. Wearing a cowboy hat, the leader of the group came forward to read his declaration, in a curt, pitiless tone:

"In response to the humiliation that too many amateur terrorists, too many assassins fearing neither God nor man, are inflicting on us, we affirm that the taking of hostages is an art. Because we believe in our profession, and because we have not forgotten John Wayne, I declare *A Martyr Idol* officially open."

He had pronounced this phrase more loudly, while his acolytes victoriously raised their Colts and swords over the prisoners, shouting:

"A Martyr Idol! A Martyr Idol!"

Then began, in an English with strong Arabic accents, the macabre explanation of the project:

"For six months, beneath the vigilant eye of our cameras, the six hostages will confront each other in a contest where they will have to sing, dance, pass tests. This program will be broadcast on the Internet, and a worldwide audience will be able to vote for the contestant of its choice. At the end of every month, the player who has received the smallest number of votes will be executed—unless the impious governments listen to our demands."

He turned towards the four men and two women crouching on the ground and concluded, in the encouraging tones of a director of a training session:

"Ladies and gentlemen, it's up to us to prove that terrorism is a fine art; it's up to you to demonstrate that every victim has a chance at survival by knowing how to fight. Prepare yourselves, concentrate; the tests will start tomorrow. Your life is in your hands. May the best one win!"

You can imagine the feeling of horror that spread throughout all democratic societies. Governments unanimously expressed their indignation at seeing the lives of innocent people reduced to this cynical game. After expressing their anger, they announced that everything would be done to wipe out the group and put an end to its activities, and to save the lives of the hostages. John Wayne's daughter came forward and expressed her incomprehension at such a connection between the Western star and this sordid production. The presidents of the main television channels outdid one another in their declarations of shock at the way a band of criminals had hijacked innocent entertainment shows. The Programs Director of a television reality network spoke of infringement and even of commercial usurpation. As a sign of resistance, the young contestants from *American Idol* joined together around Britney, the previous year's winner, to sing, hand in hand, a love song dedicated to the hostages.

According to the official declarations, everything would be done to prevent the broadcast of *A Martyr Idol* on the Internet. The difficulty of such an operation was soon apparent, however. From generation to generation, from system to counter-system, the worldwide web had become completely anarchic. The multiplication of interchanges, web hosts, sites disseminated throughout the whole planet made the Web an infinitely tangled labyrinth. It seemed impossible, even to the most knowledgeable experts, to track the very volatile—and continually modified—circuit that allowed the film of the hostages to circulate on the network. Thus the first episode of *A Martyr Idol* made it through the theoretical censorship without any difficulty. At first held back by their moral misgivings, the main television networks didn't long resist the attraction of high viewer ratings. With the consent of the various governments, they decided to broadcast some scenes "out of a concern for freedom of information"—while nonetheless censoring the most disturbing images, which were only accessible to internet users.

For the first test of this morbid competition, the disciples of John Wayne had organized a karaoke contest. Each contestant had to choose a song from the list provided by the terrorists—comprised mainly of American pop hits. He then had to interpret it in front of the camera, microphone in hand. The stage, improvised in the place of imprisonment, was sparsely defined by a backdrop bearing the star-studded colors of the armed militia. A spotlight lit up the runway, while members of the terrorist group, seated on chairs, holding their guns on their laps, served as audience. It was in these conditions that the first hostage-contestant appeared on the stage: a Korean nurse on a humanitarian assignment. She hardly knew any of the songs suggested, except for the disco hit "I Will Survive"—a fitting piece, which she started singing courageously, her eyes closed, almost without moving. Her shrill little Asian accent warped the words, while she tried to support the chorus with a few rhythmic sways. In the middle of the song, the contestant was overcome by a fit of anguish and burst into tears to the hisses of the cowboys, before she gave way to the next contestant.

Despite the scantiness of the material at hand, everything was done to recreate the illusion of a TV show. After every performance, the hostage, interviewed in intimate lighting, summed up his impressions. The terrorists themselves were playing the game; one could make out their military outfits and their gloved hands holding the microphone towards the victim, who stammered a few terrified words.

The second contestant, a German journalist, showed more conviction. After singing "Love Me Tender" with a nice vibrato, he solemnly appealed to the TV viewers to vote for him, in the name of the right to information. The most pitiful participant was definitely the divorced fifty-three-year-old Canadian department chief, who had come to the powder keg of the Near East where he had hoped to make a fortune by opening liquor stores. Arrested first by an Islamist group, he had been traded for a Kalashnikov and reclaimed by John Wayne's Conscience. Incapable of making any effort to carry a tune, barely conscious of the gravity of the situation, he was only worried about his house, which he'd bought on an installment plan, and his dog's health. After the first week, two contestants stood out from the pack: Kevin, seventeen, because he was the youngest and took an innocent pleasure in singing the hits he knew by heart, like a star; Françoise, a sixty-five-year-old Christian, because she hummed nursery rhymes "for the children" that drew tears from viewers around the world. She added that, if someone had to die, she should be the first, because of her age.

After every broadcast of an extract of *A Martyr Idol*, the news anchorman reminded the TV viewers not to take part in the vote, so as not to support the heinous blackmail of the kidnappers. Countless people, on TV, on the radio, in the newspapers, repeated it would be disgraceful to participate. The tension rose by the end of the first week, when the Allah No. 1

Network revealed the results of the karaoke test. His face still masked beneath his cowboy hat, the group leader put his left arm around the sixth contestant, winner of the competition: a Kuwaiti cook who had belted out "Sex Machine" with the grunts of a man in heat. On his other side, kneeling on the ground, head lowered in a sign of submission, was the Korean nurse, the loser of this first round. As people found out from the ensuing analyses, the Western and Asian audience had followed the orders of their governments asking them not to vote. Internet users of Arabic countries, however, had rushed to their computers; they had chosen the only contestant who belonged to their religion, and condemned this woman who was worth less than a camel.

No more was needed for Western opinion to wake up and, in each country, for a wave of national solidarity to push people to vote en masse for their own contestant, as in a sporting competition. Every round lasted a month and was made up of four tests. There were still three weeks left before the first execution. Could people accept, in the name of a principle, that the Kuwaiti would be the only survivor of this programmed massacre? The signal for resistance was given by Désiré Johnson, during the televised news show that had invited him to talk about his release from prison. On the set, a group of children had just offered the former condemned man a bouquet of violets, a reference to the flowers he had picked before smoking his last cigarette. Surrounded by little kids, he took the microphone and launched his appeal in favor of the hostages of *A Martyr Idol*:

"All you viewers know that I respect life. Thanks to your support, I was able to get out of prison. But today, other lives are in danger, and we have to support them by voting. Vote for anyone you like, but above all, vote. Even if the chances aren't equal, each little vote that you send in—for one hostage or another—will be your personal appeal in favor of life."

This message was followed by a veritable liberation of consciences. By the second week, a number of citizens began to follow openly, on their computers, the episodes of *A Martyr Idol*, choosing one contestant or another. The students of *American Idol* officially took Kevin's side: "He's not better than the others, but he's the youngest, and he has a right to the life that's before him." An association of retired people took the opposite course and started its own petition, demanding that Françoise be saved "because she's the oldest, because her selflessness has overwhelmed everyone, and because our society cannot afford to deprive itself of such a human quality."

The third week began with a giant Quiz in the course of which the six contestants had to answer culture-related questions. The hostages still seemed just as terrified in front of the camera; but, in the free world, they were now seen as stars. The media told their stories; the tabloids collected secrets about each of them, along with personal photos; *A Martyr Idol* would have become the most beloved of public competitions if, as it was reaching its fourth week, it weren't common knowledge that, barring a miracle, one of the contestant's throats would be cut within a week.

9

For a good twenty minutes, the police van idled in the traffic jam on Victory Boulevard. Sitting between two policemen, I can see the passersby through the bullet-proof window. They're returning from work, waiting for the red light; they seem satisfied with living in this history-laden city—even though the present era requires certain compromises. Many of them are holding handkerchiefs to their faces; other have picked up one of the masks on sale on the sidewalks for one eurollar, like a coffee filter you stretch over your mouth and nose, with an elastic band. Dominating this human swarm, an immense poster covers the front of the town hall, announcing the event all citizens can take part in till Monday:

5th WEEKEND OF PURE AIR

When I was a city employee, I remember writing up a little analysis, thanks to confidential figures provided by the pollution control center. It emerged curiously that, during the weekends of pure air—when the mayor's teams visit the neighborhoods to celebrate "the city that breathes"—the degree of ozone and carbon dioxide is multiplied by an average of 1.5 per cent over the rest of the year (when this rate is already above the maximum allowed for good health). To mark the event, our mayor had decided, in fact, to ban traffic from a dozen boulevards and fast lanes, which forced cars to pile up in all the other routes in huge traffic jams. They could have banned all traffic; instead, they were content to "advise against" it. This recommendation had no influence whatsoever on the people concerned, especially the suburbanites who use their cars precisely... to go to pure-air days.

Set up in the traffic-free lanes, a number of street shows try to make the public more aware by means of various entertainments. I can see the list of events in my mind's eye, from a memo:

1) Installation of parks for bicycles, rollerblades and scooters at intersections;

2) Welcoming the public to "oxygen cafés," where the consumer will find documentaries on air and its composition; he can also learn how to read and analyze pollution levels;

3) Every hour, release, by children, of multicolored balloons filled with pure air.

These were followed by other points that I've forgotten, until the closing celebration on Sunday night, during which the mayor ritually utters his grand oration on *Air and Life*.

During this weekend, the closings of the boulevards led to a formidable increase in pollution; but the celebrations of air also favor an aggravation of atmospheric pollution *throughout the entire year*, since the meetings organized during a weekend allow the municipality and the media to neglect the subject until the next Monday. After showing their involvement in the degradation of conditions of life on the planet, they can return to other preoccupations, like the urgency of economic recovery, the positive signs of the automobile industry, the "good news" coming from Asia where consumerism is quickly reaching double-digit levels. One could object that the degradation of the environment is aggravated by economic recovery, the production of cars, and double-digit growth in Asian countries; but the rule is to remain optimistic; to rejoice on one hand and to worry slightly on the other, with a good measure of sense and responsibility.

As I think about it, I find I'm returning to this neighborhood without any nostalgia. Everything I loved in this city, when I came here for the first time, seems to have disappeared today, replaced by major franchises: the cheese stores, the fishmongers and craftsmen's studios, the bars at night and the restaurants in the early morning, the dark streets and the dusty secondhand shops, the neighborhood movie theaters...In their place, I see almost nothing but clothing stores, clothing stores, clothing stores. The city is proudly filling up with the commonplace specialties you can find from one end of the planet to the other: fast-food restaurants for poor people and not so poor people (in which case fast food is disguised as traditional cuisine); a rhythm of life completely regulated by weekends and work schedules; general closing of bistros after midnight; no smoking anywhere; children's rights, which are increasing everywhere (in front of the school near where I live, at a little crossroads without any cars, they have planted no less than eight red lights). In short, the self-conscious comforts of a provincial city dumped onto this city that thought of itself as one of the greatest cities in the world. I perceive this in my police van, and I tell myself that when it comes down to it, I'm not losing much; I'll just have to be brave.

According to what I learned, the traffic conditions, during this fifth weekend of pure air, will be even more aggravated by the demonstration that's been organized in Republic Square in favor of Kevin from *A Martyr Idol*. The media fear clashes with the procession of retired people who want to save Françoise's life, and the procession of journalists who favor the German reporter.... Kevin's supporters, however, benefit from a key ally, Désiré Johnson, who will walk at the head of the demonstrators. According to him, the most important thing is to "save youth, which is future life." Ever since his liberation, he has become a kind of prophet, his photo plastered on all the city's walls. The two guards sitting in the police van on my left and right are among his supporters. The younger one, an Indonesian with a shaved head, was explaining just now to his colleague, a tall Chilean woman chewing gum:

"Really, I felt so much better when he wrote those words with flowers: 'Long live life.' What strength for a guy who's about to die!"

"Me, I refuse to believe Désiré killed a cop. Just from his smile, you can see he respects life.... Not like you, you son of a bitch!" the guard retorted, tapping me on the elbow with an almost friendly laugh.

I could have kept quiet, but I spoke up—a way for me to prepare for the upcoming meeting:

"At least his case has let us think about the right to smoke, in this country."

"That's what I find hard to understand!" the Indonesian retorted. "How can he defend both the right to life and the right to cigarettes?"

"The right to life," I replied, "is also the right to taste dangerous pleasures. But there is one point I disagree with Johnson about...."

"Oh yeah? Wanna tell us?" the Chilean asked with that familiarity that sometimes brings guards closer to prisoners.

"Yes, it's when he says it's better to kill a fifty-year-old man than an old man, a woman, or a child!"

Immediately, her smile transformed into a grimace:

"It surprises me that a pervert like you would rather attack the weak and the innocent!"

"No, it's a question of severity. For me, children are incomplete beings with very basic reactions; they don't think about anything except eating, crying, controlling in an almost mechanical way. As for old people, death is already familiar to them, and they're waiting for its rest. Not to mention women: they have obtained equality, and I don't see why we should grant them any special privileges.... No, in my opinion, it's the adult man, the forty- or fifty-year-old man who needs the most support, because of the way everyone scorns him. He still loves life, but he feels death approaching; from his intellectual faculties, he thinks he is at the top of his form, but his boss is already thinking about getting rid of him; everywhere, younger individuals are waiting to take his place. His ex-wife thinks of him as a nuisance, just good for paying the alimony. His own children think he's completely out of it. As for his secretary, she's waiting for the first crooked smile to accuse him of 'sexual harassment' and make him pay.... In his life, everything's reaching its peak and collapsing. I see no more fragile symbol of the human condition."

"And that's why you want to hurt children?"

"I've never set out to hurt them. I ignore them. Nothing about them attracts me. They're embryos, just barely confronted with the richness of the language, the subtlety of the social

game, with the joys and suffering of love. Look at sick children
who die consoling their parents, with the acceptance of people
who haven't gotten to know life yet. Death is just a slight passage for them, almost superficial. Whereas for the adult in full
maturity, the terror when he's faced with the abyss, the inten-
sity of his nostalgia, are infinite. From all that I deduce that, if
you absolutely had to make this kind of choice, it would be
preferable, out of humanity, to kill a young child—and, even
better, a baby—than a mature man."

Once again, it seemed as if I were acknowledging my guilt.
The indifference I expressed for children seemed to be strangely expressed—in the coarse minds of my guards—by an irresistible attraction for little girls. The logic of my case seems
impossible to convey; sensibility refuses to admit my innocence, when reason establishes its proof.

Latifa noticed this too, during the meeting with the mayor
she had been requesting for weeks. Each time, the mayor's
office had flatly refused her, admitting complete indifference
for the near past when the municipal team had appreciated my
advice. From all that, there remained only the cold refusal to
speak to a *criminal against children*, and even a reproachful tone
in the secretaries' voices, as if my crime hurt the city's image.
But nothing could discourage Latifa, not even the sordid search
for which I had returned handcuffed to my home; Sarko rub-
bing against my legs like a wretched thing, while the police

officers turned the house upside-down looking for photos, videos, or traces of my crimes. They found nothing, but I returned to prison.

Convinced that support from high up could save me, Latifa wanted absolutely to demonstrate my innocence to the mayor. To manage this, she ended up calling the mayor's office using her journalist pseudonym, and she suggested a "major interview" for a women's magazine. Immediately doors were opened. Three days later, she got her meeting with the friend of women, who came to the lobby himself to find her and asked her to follow him to his office.

Without giving herself away, Latifa got out her notebook and began with some general questions. His eyes twinkling, his tone confidential, a lock of grey hair falling artistically over his forehead, the mayor seemed happy to pour out his heart, deliver a few secrets of his political itinerary (honesty, stringency, absence of interest in money, and above all "a real curiosity about people"). After about fifteen minutes, in this climate of friendship and confidence, my companion finally asked the question that was burning on her lips:

"Tell me, Mr. Mayor, I'd like to come back to the unfortunate affair of that 'technical adviser' who was recently imprisoned...."

Even before she could finish asking her question, my former boss took on a serious look, expressing the accepted opinion:

"Horrible! Disgusting! To do that to a little kid, within our own walls: I take this affair as a personal failure. Are you aware that, according to the Juvenile Division, fourteen other children could have been victims of his fondling? The city has sued, and I will do everything in my power so this guy won't escape his punishment."

"When I mentioned the 'unfortunate affair,' I was thinking, Mr. Mayor...that there's no serious proof against the accused man, whose life has been shattered by a crime that he formally denies."

"Criminals always deny! Do you have to be reminded that this guy smoked a cigarette inside the premises, to the detriment of the health of the children? That says a lot about his manner of thinking!"

"But as hard proof, it's pretty thin!"

Suddenly, the mayor realized that she was defending my cause, and the tone of the conversation changed. So as not to compromise his interview with the women's magazine, he began to choose his words carefully:

"Listen, ma'am, I don't know why you're interested in this guy, but I'm going to tell you what I think about it—with the understanding that starting from now, this conversation will stay between us, off the record...."

As she explained to me in the visitor's room, Latifa felt the aggressiveness in his voice. He explained, word for word:

"This man worked here for years. I know him and I know that he's a pervert! I'm going to give you an example: when I tried to purify the air in our streets and return the city to its inhabitants, this gentleman gathered and provided suspicious analyses trying to prove that the atmosphere was literally poisoned."

"That might have been done to help you."

"Sure! Me, I'd rather be served by emphasizing the good sides of my actions! One more thing: When I went to the trouble of transforming half of Administration City into a daycare center, when I had the renovations done, when I demolished the apartments that were provided for municipal employees; when I built new rooms, when I set up the nursery-spaces, youth-spaces," (listening to the mayor, you'd have thought he had done all this himself, with his toolbox) "...in short, when I carried out all this work for the common good, this gentleman—who, by the way, is not stupid!—found nothing better to do than join a minority of employees who claimed to be annoyed in their work by the presence of children. You heard right: DISTURBED BY CHILDREN.... When you reach that point, something isn't right. What's more, someone told me he actually insulted the little ones in the hallways. So I began to think that this individual might be an enemy and a danger in the midst of my own team; which is hard for me to admit!"

"And what if I tell you he's innocent?"

At these words, he looked annoyed and made a gesture to wave aside this hypothesis:

"Young lady, the word of a child is at stake! And my goal

is to restore speech to the children. So I am going to tell you a secret: you know that every month I meet with the Municipal Council of Children, which enlightens us on their wishes in the transformations of this city...."

He had resumed his politician's tone:

"Well, I have called for a special meeting of this Council, which will allow our young citizens to overcome the trauma connected with this affair. Because children do talk amongst themselves and, sometimes, the facts get stretched...."

"Are you suggesting that they don't always tell the truth?"

"I don't feel like joking, my dear lady.... I am therefore going to form a 'Children's Court' that will pass a verdict on this man's case; purely symbolically, of course. I asked the courts to grant us the presence of the accused man during the meeting so that the victims can put a face to the harm that was done to them."

Latifa was shaken by the violence of this procedure; but this supposedly human, benevolent man justified himself with a semi-scientific, serious:

"Such a step has been approved by the psychological aid unit that was set up after the assault on Amandine...."

He had uttered the name "Amandine" as if she were his own daughter. He had nothing more to add.

*

As I get out of the police van, two guards from Administration City join the Indonesian and the Chilean. Now I'm waiting patiently under their surveillance, in the vestibule at the entrance to the Assembly. A TV screen allows us to follow the opening remarks. Perched at the rostrum in the amphitheater, the mayor takes out a T-shirt with Désiré's slogan on it: "Long Live Life." Seated next to him, the president of the meeting is a little girl about twelve years old wearing lipstick and a severe suit. In the rows of the council members about a hundred kids from four to fourteen are sitting. Backpacks and snacks have been put on the tables; sometimes a child begins to wail, and its mother comes down from the audience section to calm it down, then goes back to rejoin the big people who don't have the right to intervene during the assembly. Some pre-teens are wearing sexy clothes; especially the girls in tight T-shirts that emphasize their growing chests and let their little tummies peek out, but we'll skip over that.... We are here for indecent exposure committed *on* a child and not *by* a child, as the mayor of the city gravely explains:

"My dear colleagues" (he utters these words without smiling), "as you know, we are gathered in this special meeting after the horrible assault committed by an employee of Administration City on your comrade Amandine. I would like first of all to reassure you by emphasizing strongly that the man responsible *is no longer employed at this office* and that he is now behind bars...."

He has the fervent gaze, the serious tone that I knew him to have during meetings; still that perfect honesty in examining my case:

"I am aware, however, that that is not enough. Amandine hasn't come to the daycare center for several weeks; I call her regularly but she is still shocked; the path will be a long one, for her and for her family, before she can resume a normal life. In solidarity with them—and with the fourteen children who may have been victims of fondling—it seemed necessary to me to call a meeting of this Municipal Youth Council, transformed today into a Children's Court. I wanted you to be able to express yourselves on this affair; say how you have lived through this trauma; speak to remember, speak to understand, and speak to forget. In the course of this meeting, I am very pleased that I have obtained—thanks to my good relations with the Department of Justice—the presence of the accused. You will be able to tell him to his face the harm he has done to you. As for me, I will not impose myself any further: this council is your own, not mine. I will go and join the public in the back of the room and let you take the floor, Madam President, to conduct this meeting."

He turns warmly to the girl, who was beginning to suck her thumb; she quickly sits up and takes on a stiff pose:

"Thank you, Mr. Mayor, for that introduction."

The little girl then undertakes to read carefully the text in front of her, syllable by syllable, with childlike hesitations:

"As we decided in a pre...preliminary meeting, I am going to summon the man we have to judge, before we give the floor to the pro...prosecutor, then to the lawyer in charge of ensuring his de...defense—for the children's court respects the de... democratic forms of Justice."

After this last phrase, she shouts:

"Guards, bring in the accused!"

The two City Hall guards gesture for me to get up; they push the door of the Assembly open and enter with me without leaving me for an instant—in case I decide to rush again at a little girl. A little bewildered, handcuffs on my wrists, I sweep my eyes over the assembly room, which looks like any other political room with its tiers for the delegates and, at the top, the vast balcony for spectators.... Except that the delegates have kid's heads, unformed faces chewing sweets; sticky mouths that have just lost their baby teeth; upturned noses and unfinished hands moving over their consoles to take notes—as if real policies in the service of the nation were at stake. Some boys are wearing grey suits, bought for the occasion by their parents, who plan on their going into administrative careers. The biggest boys have pink cheeks but shaved heads and earrings. Walking in front of them, I fear a wave of hisses, gum and pencils being thrown, but they keep a solemn silence, an adult attitude that contrasts with their puerile features.

"I call to the stand the prosecutor Jonathan Leduc," the President shouts.

A blond boy emerges from the seats; he is about twelve years old, and his skull—despite his young age—seems to be balding, like that of a senior official. His very strict haircut gives him that egghead look characteristic of office chiefs— reinforced by rectangular glasses that are a little too wide and by the tie knotted around his neck. After joining me at the bar, the child takes the floor like a young ace lawyer, and utters his speech without notes:

"My dear colleagues, I remember, when I was little, seeing an episode of Mickey Mouse in which Pluto, the hardened bachelor, claimed not to like children.... In the beginning of this story, he grumbles continually and rails against a band of young puppies who, however, want only to play with him. And then, a reversal: the young puppies end up ignoring him; and then Pluto begins to spy on them, follow them with a curious and frustrated avidity. This mixture of attraction and jealousy will only subside when Pluto meets a female dog and becomes a father in turn...."

Jonathan Leduc swallows his saliva and goes on:

"I thought several times about this episode when I learned about the sad affair of Amandine—whom I don't have the privilege of knowing personally, since she is much younger than me and was still in kindergarten when I was already in the big kids' daycare...."

Oratorical gestures accompany his words:

"Yes, I thought about Pluto as I studied the case of this man who, when asked why he assaulted a defenseless little girl, answered with this gross denial: 'It's not true. Anyway I'm not interested in children!'"

He waits for silence before pointing out, in a common-sense tone:

"Obviously, there is a certain link between those who aren't interested in children, and those who are too interested in them; between those who run away from us and those who feel an irresistible, sometimes unnatural impulse towards us."

After outlining the psychological framework of the affair, the prosecutor moves on to the question of proof:

"You might think I exaggerate if I state that the accused man is guided by a pathological hatred of children. To prove this to you, I would like to call to the stand a witness we found—with the help of the services of Administration City—thanks to the video footage kept by the Transportation Agency. I know that the word of an adult is not always reliable; but here it's a question of an old lady, a kind of grandmother," (he smiles) "to whom I ask you to give your attention."

The President of the meeting makes a sign and we see, in the back of the room, a woman about sixty-five years old get up and come down to the stand. I don't identify her right away but, when she begins to testify, I recognize her harsh voice, and I remember this lady in the company of another woman, in the back of the bus—on a day I was returning home from work, especially nervous. Facing the audience, she declares:

"As surprising as this might seem, while the children were sitting quite calmly in the bus, this gentleman shouted: 'Will you look at these little oafs....' Or something like that. When no one was asking for anything, it was as if he wanted to force the children to get up! As if they weren't tired, the angels, after a day at the well-ventilated center...."

I exclaim:

"When I was little, my dear lady, children got up to give their seats to big people!"

"Defendant, you do not have the stand," the President cuts in curtly.

On his side, Prosecutor Leduc addresses the assembly with an ironic aside:

"I am unaware what era the defendant is referring to. But you have before you the example of the ravages accomplished by the kind of education they had, *at that famous time!*"

A wave of applause rises from the assembly. The president asks for silence before returning the floor to Jonathan Leduc, who proceeds immediately to give his conclusion, holding his glasses by the tips of his fingers before replacing them on his nose:

"We do not want to interfere in the legal process. As you know, this court is purely consultative, and the adult court alone takes account of the crimes of the defendant.... Nonetheless, I am convinced that this man presents a real danger. To recover from their suffering, Amandine and her family (not to mention the fourteen other presumed victims) need him to undergo a fair punishment. But because I am a child and I have faith in life, I would also not like any adult to be lost for good. That is why I express the wish that the court envisage an appropriate treatment that will help the defendant to get over his nightmares...."

"You're my only nightmare, you snot-nosed brat!"

I couldn't restrain myself; so now the prosecutor can conclude, with a half-smile:

"I told you so...."

A round of stifled laughter goes through the assembly while the President again withdraws her thumb from her red lips and announces the intervention for the defense. A little eleven-year-old girl comes down to the bar, in a navy blue blouse and skirt. Two long braids fall onto her shoulders; she looks like a goody-two-shoes and takes the floor with a quiet voice:

"In this interesting cartoon evoked just now by Mr. Leduc, I would bring to mind a different aspect: the moment when

Pluto finally finds serenity after he has started a family. I think, in fact, that it would be unreasonable to treat the case of a prisoner like this without taking into account the suffering of not being a father, the absence of contact with little ones, which ends up being translated into a kind of aversion. On this point, other testimonies deserve to be heard."

This nice little nun has no intention of questioning my guilt; she is only trying to pass me off as a potential friend of children, a dad disappointed at not being a dad. I would never have imagined, before, the base methods to which this court is ready to resort in order to force me to pay. For to support her theory, the lawyer announces:

"The person who will come to the bar knows the defendant better than anyone; she knows the father's heart that is hidden beneath the heart of stone...."

A sob rises up in my throat when I see, in the back of the room, the beautiful, slim silhouette of Latifa stand up, her features ravaged by fatigue and suffering. While she looks at me with her large sad eyes, empty of their usual energy, I understand the blackmail they have subjected her to: "Either you testify, you play the game of the court, you enlighten us about this man's problem with children, and we will plead attenuating circumstances; or you refuse, and we won't answer for the consequences." Forgetting our dreams of happiness, outside the constraints of our time, Latifa came to testify before this court because it's her last chance. Seemingly very tired, she places a hand on the bar and begins to answer the questions:

"How long have you been living with this man?"

"Ten years."

"Were you happy together?"

"Perfectly happy. We lived as two lovers, cultivating the taste for pleasure."

"Isn't there something a little selfish, in that?"

"Perhaps, but we were happy that way."

"And you never thought about sharing this happiness with children?"

Latifa pauses before looking at me despairingly, as if she were betraying us both:

"It's true, I thought about it sometimes; but he didn't want any."

A murmur went through the audience. The young lawyer turns around to emphasize this major revelation:

"I think that the court is beginning to understand that, behind this whole affair, there is the tragedy of a couple...."

She again questions Latifa:

"And, how should I say...you never noticed, in your companion, a suspicious behavior with children, little girls, little boys?"

My companion almost shouts:

"No, never, I swear it! I am positive that whole story is a lie!"

Other shouts are heard in the room. Several parents have stood up, crying out:

"That's disgraceful to say such things! Our children told us! Bitch!"

I take advantage of the commotion to ask Latifa:

"Why did you come into this trap?"

"It's all I could do, darling. Ms. Pataki assured me. Forgive me."

The President raps her gavel:

"Silence, please...."

Latifa whispers to me in a sob:

"I'm exhausted, I can't take anymore. You have to try to understand me, but I'm going to stay away for a little bit. I hope everything works out for you."

The lawyer has taken the floor again:

"One last question, ma'am: do you still want to have a child?"

"Yes, I think so," Latifa replies.

"And do you want to have a child...with the defendant?"

My pretty companion is silent again before sighing, lowering her eyes:

"I think that's no longer possible."

She reaches the exit without turning back. My heart broken, I remain like a dead man, abandoned by everyone, while my young advocate comes to her conclusion:

"Obviously, the guilt seems difficult to question, but I would like to plead extenuating circumstances, to remind you that this man was—apparently—a good companion. I think experts should examine his case and bring to light the damaged mechanism that has prevented him from becoming a father and that has led him to this insane behavior with Amandine and a dozen other children."

"Bitch!"

Silence. I had spoken in a moderate tone, but clear enough to be heard by the whole room. So, to confirm what I had just said, I gather together my strength, banish my sadness, and turn to the President, asking very calmly:

"Madam President, I would like this bitch to shut up so that I can have the floor, as is my right, seemingly, during the meeting."

The little girl at the rostrum makes an angry child's face. She is visibly searching for her words before replying, childlike:

"You don't have to insult my girlfriend!"

Then she resumes in a solemn, but hesitant, voice:

"But our court is demo... cratic, and you have the right to speak for a few minutes."

"Thank you, Madam President. I will not take long."

I turn towards the audience, keeping as courteous and measured a tone as I can:

"All I have to say to you, band of ridiculous kids...."

At these words, hisses erupt, while the young President bangs her gavel:

●

"Silence, please."

I continue, determined to go to the end:

"All I have to say to you, bunch of little snot-nosed brats, pile of larvae who won't become anything; all I'm going to explain to you, band of brats overdosed on TV, susceptible to all the stupid things they inject into your ears, with the help of compliant parents...."

More hisses, this time from the adult section:

"All I want to make you understand, little runts who'd do better to work quietly at school, wait for people to let you speak, raise your hands to ask permission, be punished for your base tricks and rewarded for your rare good actions...."

Silence again. Curiously, a few smiles begin to illuminate the childlike faces. This flood of invectives impresses them, but only the way a circus performance from another era would. They're listening to me now, blissful, idiotic, delighted that I'm continuing this furious speech:

"All I have to say to you, is that I never could have touched that little idiot Amandine, no more than I could the fourteen others; because I don't know of anything less interesting than a child. For me you're not even human beings yet, but little animals that I would never hurt—so long as they stay in their cages and don't disturb my adult life, which is infinitely more difficult, richer, and more problematic than yours, and, when it is wasted, infinitely more beautiful and tragic than your baby actions. For me, you don't exist, the fourteen kids don't exist, Amandine doesn't exist. In short, I don't give a fuck about that little asshole, and I'd never dream of fucking her little hole."

After Latifa's departure, no sense of propriety is holding me back. I just want to inform these creatures of their objective uselessness; and the children are contemplating me now as if I were an extremely curious kind of animal. In the first row, a fat boy about ten years old with a gaping mouth is slobbering a little. He seems so stupid that—it comes to me now—I shouldn't even bother to explain anything to him. He's looking at me like one of those innumerable attractions they've made available to him since infancy. And as this idea becomes increasingly clearer to me, I suddenly interrupt myself in my rant, thinking of the absurdity of this situation, and remind them, sighing:

"All I did is smoke a cigarette."

The silence continues. My lawyer, who seems to want to do me in at any price, observes:

"Still. That's not respecting the health of children much!"

"But why do you want me to respect children? They're the ones that should respect me!"

At these words, a new round of laughter rises up and fills the room, although I thought I was talking with some kind of good sense. Already the young prosecutor is returning to the bar to conclude:

"Sir, we'll pass over the question of your guilt, which concerns the adult court. We'll even pass over the cigarette: You may indeed be the most depraved of men, but that shouldn't prevent you—it seems to me—from showing a few human emotions. And you can still attenuate your guilt by declaring, at least once, your respect for children, your support for growing life. Why not take your inspiration from the magnificent attitude of Désiré Johnson, whom everyone thought was a criminal but who could say these words: 'Long live life'? By this gesture, he deserved his freedom. What are you going to do to deserve your own?"

That is the question. I could explain how I disagree with Johnson: This worship of innocence that constitutes, in my opinion, a logical mistake. But with theories like that I would only dig myself in deeper, and I understand that I can do nothing but keep quiet. Turning my head to the President, who is looking at me and sucking her thumb, I say wearily:

"I want to go now!"

Surrounded by my guards, I leave the room without adding anything.

When the door closes behind me, I recognize the silhouette of my lawyer in the lobby—the real one, Maren Pataki. She had promised to come and, once again, she arrives late. But for the first time, this observation raises my spirits. Defended by an incompetent, I don't have any chance of getting out of this; but after having lost everything (my job, my profession, my wife, my honor...), her mediocrity seems to me an objective element, a simple given of the human condition. I am not the victim of a conspiracy, but of a natural accumulation of stupidity. What's more, as usual, Maren Pataki doesn't feel the slightest guilt. She contents herself with saying:

"You were very bad!"

"Really?"

"Yes, really! That's why I can't manage to defend you. The children are right: help me, do some kind of gesture, like Désiré!"

So it's up to me to help her; up to me to prove myself innocent, as her most famous client did before me.

10

For a month, Désiré Johnson's last cigarette had held TV viewers breathless; by the end of April, the promotional market had reached its highest point, thanks to the condemned man's imagination. Then after the presidential pardon, the worldwide audience had almost fallen back into lethargy. Advertisers were already planning on reducing their budgets when the horrible conspiracy of *A Martyr Idol* had brought the great mass of citizens back to their TV screens, making ratings rise to numbers that hadn't been seen since the last World Cup of soccer. A few polemicists were quick to discuss a conspiracy theory, even if it meant raising outrageous questions: Wasn't this unlikely terrorist group the result of media manipulation? Wasn't it objectively serving the large communication companies? Right away, public outcry had rejected the notion of such cynicism playing with the lives of hostages. By joining the campaign of opinion in favor of the victims and by calling for everyone to vote "with his heart," Désiré had once and for all shut up the experts of disinformation.

It was in this context, one month after the start of the show, that the name of the loser of the first round was finally revealed. Although he had appeared completely at ease during the modern dance test, to general surprise it was the German journalist—the very one who had kept repeating to the camera: "I came to this region for information. If you kill me, you kill freedom of the press." Had the indignation expressed by his colleagues (who, throughout the whole world, fought for his liberation, convinced that his profession made him deserve a special indulgence) played against him? Did the audience think that this reporter on special assignment knew the risks he was running? Or that a forty-year-old man had to go through it first, rather than a teenager, a woman or an old person? The opinion specialists in any case all agreed in observing that, this time, the contestant's origin and religion had played no determining role in the voting. Whether they were from the West, the Third World, Asia or the Arabic countries, a majority of voters chose this man as the loser, while the young Kevin and the old Françoise were still in the lead. After four weeks of tests, opinion seemed more "mature," exercising its own choices without giving in to outside considerations. At this point the game was becoming really interesting, when everything froze in one terrible question.

Were the disciples of John Wayne going to carry out their threat, or would they respond to appeals for clemency? Every morning, public opinion hoped to learn news of the journalist's pardon—even if some sadistic byways of the human spirit were expecting the worst to take place on television. A week later came the announcement of the execution, and the broadcasting of the images cooled the ardor of those who had gotten to the point of watching the show as if it were a game. After the victim was made to kneel down and his hands tied behind his back, the chief of the terrorist group himself cut his throat in front of the camera and then held up the terrified, bloody head. The unbearable brutality of the clip led to a return of scruples. Internet forums announced a boycott of this morbid serial; most television networks refused to show *A Martyr Idol*, preferring to let the secret services act discreetly for the liberation of the prisoners.

Everything might have faded away if it were not for the appearance of a new press release announcing that a man—imprisoned for the sexual harassment of fifteen minors—wanted "to hand himself over to the terrorists, in exchange for the life of a hostage." The news item summarized the sordid affair that had led this individual to prison, where he was awaiting his judgment: indecent exposure towards a little five-year-old girl, and suspicions about the organization of a perverted network of which the children at Administration City were the alleged victims. Nothing to inspire pity.... By shattering a little girl's dreams, this man had also destroyed his own life, lost his job and his companion. He had then sent his lawyer, Ms. Maren Pataki, this offer, in which he wrote: "By acting this way, I hope I can psychologically support the little Amandine, help her to chase away her demons, and redeem myself by saving the life of an innocent person."

It was the coup de théâtre that no one was expecting. When she revealed the announcement to the press, Ms. Pataki seemed overwhelmed with real joy. Once again, her client had come up with the right idea! Even if it was formulated by an abject criminal, this proposition could change the evolution of *A Martyr Idol*. The scoop was broadcast by all the networks, and public opinion again began its debates. Some thought the trade should be allowed; others refused to violate the rules of the courts, even to spare the life of a hostage. The former point of view prevailed pretty clearly, as François, a thirty-three year old systems analyst, summarized during a televised news program: "This guy did some horrible things. He's a sick man. But he wants to redeem himself by saving an innocent life, even if it means losing his head. That means he still has a little human dignity. Why not give him the chance?"

Questioned on the Ooh La La Network, Amandine's mother was not of that opinion. Furious in her leatherette pants and purple jacket, she said indignantly: "That's not what will help my daughter get over it, after what she has lived through! Today, she no longer talks, she doesn't want to go to school anymore. And I haven't even gotten the damages yet. It's always the little ones who suffer! The important thing is that this monster pay for what he owes society, and that Amandine has a little comfort to help with her convalescence."

As if to respond to this apprehension, Ms. Pataki announced that before any possible transfer of the accused to the Near East, he would hand over all his property to the courts. The position of principle still remained, which was adopted by the political authorities at the beginning of the affair: "We do not negotiate with hostage takers." It was an official point of view combatted more and more openly by the main victims' associations: "A bastard for an innocent person— yes!", shouted the pamphlets distributed at streetcorners. The decisive event in this debate was the declaration by an ecu- menical group of bishops, imams, and rabbis, "inviting the civil and religious authorities to do everything possible to allow this gesture of charity that could save the innocent and purify the guilty." In a context where the weight of different churches always carried more influence than that of state gov- ernments, this message of peace carried the day.

Then people realized that no one had given a thought to the opinion of the hostage takers. How could they hope that a band of killers would liberate an innocent person in exchange for a criminal? Would they take the risk of placing themselves in danger by undertaking this trade? The question remained unanswered until a message from the terrorists, on the Allah

No. 1 Network, finally made their official position clear: in response to the appeal from the religious authorities, they wanted to show to the world the humanism of their cause, which was mainly intended to improve the status of terrorism; therefore, they accepted the principle of an exchange. Taking into account all these facts, the President of the Republic signified, in a televised interview, why he finally had come over to the opinion of the religious experts; the transaction could take place during the second half of June. The exact date was not divulged.

A few months later, in an exclusive interview on the Our Lord Network, Monsignor El Ghoury revealed how those tragic hours had unfurled.

*

The operation had taken place in the middle of the desert, a few miles away from the Syrian border. After the religious personalities had given the green light, a Christian militia established in the region had agreed to protect the expedition. The secret service would transport the person in question to Beirut. In the plan accepted by the different parties, it was agreed that a representative of the Maronite Church would then accompany the prisoner to the point of exchange. Monsignor El Ghoury, a Catholic prelate used to these kinds of negotiations, was in charge of ensuring the mission's success, in keeping with the taste for espionage he had developed over the years, concealed beneath his ecclesiastical haberdashery.

After he arrived at the Beirut airport escorted by two plainclothes officers, the volunteer was led, under escort of the Lebanese police, to a chapel belonging to the diocese. The automobile rolled through the high white wall of the building where secret affairs of religious diplomacy were decided. As he got out of the car, handcuffs on his wrists, the prisoner had the feeling of entering, for the first time since his arrest, a protected place, far from the pressure of interrogations. A fountain bubbled in the middle of the garden which smelled sweetly of jasmine. Scarcely had he left the car than he saw on the front steps a prelate in a black suit, his face tanned, a little silver cross on his jacket lapel, and a cigarette in his mouth. Coming down the steps with an old fighter's gait, Msgr. El Ghoury walked towards his guest as if he were receiving a distinguished visitor:

"Greetings! It is wonderful to meet you," he said in a coarse voice, rolling his r's.

Without taking the time to greet the representatives of the secret service or those from the Lebanese police, he embraced the prisoner as if to thank him for coming, then announced:

"We'll leave tomorrow morning, but I'd like to chat a little with you. We will have a cup of tea and pray. Gentlemen, would you be so kind as to remove these handcuffs?"

"Hey! This is no hotel!" exclaimed one of the men who wasn't at all on the same page.

The priest turned towards him, furious:

"According to the agreements that were signed, the prisoner is now in my hands. I will treat him in the way that seems suitable to me, even as a distinguished guest, if I like. At dawn, I will head out with the soldiers of the Christ the King Militia to go to the place of transaction. You will wait here for me to return; an apartment is at your disposal, on the other side of the courtyard. From now on, we have nothing more to say to each other."

Freed from his handcuffs, the prisoner followed the prelate to a room with a high ceiling, framed with religious portraits of bishops and patriarchs. The two men sat down on either side of a massive wooden table. A nun entered the room with a tray and served tea; then the man of the church got out a pack of filterless Gauloises from his pocket and held one out to his interlocutor:

"I know that, in this kind of business, extravagant lies and unfortunate exaggerations can shatter a man's life. It's a painful experience that we in the Church are very familiar with."

To go to the Near East in this intense end-of-June heat, the prisoner had donned a light-colored suit and a light shirt. They had let him use his personal wardrobe—as if the courts themselves took the choice of his outfit seriously, since it could have some importance in the televised game. As he was plunging into the nightmare, the former city employee nonetheless felt strangely free, for the first time in weeks. Without saying anything, he swallowed several puffs of cigarette smoke and exhaled into the space around him, making smoke rings. The priest was still talking:

"The children in rich countries seem very sensitive to me, these days!"

By minimizing the crime against children, it was as if he wanted to obtain a confession. The prisoner gestured with annoyance:

"Maybe.... Except I never touched any little girl!"

"If you're innocent, why give yourself up as a hostage?"

"Because they never let me prove my innocence for a second!"

"You could have waited for the trial."

"It would have taken place behind closed doors, so as not to 'traumatize' the girl. My lawyer is convinced there's nothing left to hope for. Let's say I'm doing this gesture for honor!"

"You can still change your mind."

"I've lost everything in any case. And also...I have an idea in the back of my mind. Because of that Johnson affair, you know? When he wrote 'Long live life' with his bouquet of flowers."

"That was clever of him," the priest observed. "He became popular. With a little luck, he'll soon be proven innocent and even compensated."

"All the better for him. Anyway, I wanted to answer his theory: 'I'll never hurt an old man, a woman, a child....'"

" '...or a handicapped person!' Yes, I remember. It's a very old principle, you know: 'Women and children first!'"

"Okay, but in this world that's so preoccupied with protecting the weak, doesn't a man, an ordinary forty- or fifty-year-old man, deserve a little compassion? That's the question I got to when I was wondering which one of the hostages of *A Martyr Idol* I'd rather save, if I could."

"How were you able to watch the show?"

"The prison warden let me go onto the Web so I could prepare.... So I proceeded by elimination, beginning with that idiot Kevin who wins all the tests by showing off his youth. After all, the youngest is also the most unaware, and probably the one who is least afraid of death.... And then I eliminated Françoise, the old lady who wants to die first, as if she already had one foot in the grave."

"That's a little harsh, what you're saying."

"No, it's logical, it's almost scientific, Father. The journalist didn't last long either, in my mind. There's someone who looked for what he got, by running to the site to cover the story. Obviously, the antipathy he aroused might have made me sympathetic. But his execution didn't leave me any time."

"You could have chosen the Korean nurse."

"Of course, she is moving, in her humanitarian mission. But she seems drawn by the world's misfortune—she can't get close enough to wounds and suffering. Now she's had her fill.... And don't even talk to me about that Arab, convinced he was spared because the terrorists are Muslim like him. No, frankly, if their God wants blood, they should start by taking his own!"

He seemed to reflect for another minute before concluding:

"In fact, one single person in the group seemed worthy to me to continue living: that Canadian who was stupid enough to hope to get rich by starting a liquor store chain in a country that's in the middle of an Islamic war. He's the average clueless contestant, the perfect representative of the human species in its minimal, mulish, unmoving aspect—and, because of that, its mysteriously sublime quality.... When the others are trying to touch the public with human emotions, he talks about his dog—his 'only companion' since his wife left him. Me too, I had a dog.... And I came to like this man, this unattractive man, this man who's neither young nor old and who's incapable of singing, devoid of all the necessary qualities for showbiz. If I didn't choose him, he'd have absolutely no chance to escape."

A gleam of light had appeared in the priest's eyes. There was something ironic and mocking that went well with his badly shaved beard, his cigarette, and his yellow fingers; something that brought him closer to his interlocutor. He asked:

"How do you hope to get your message across?"

The volunteer raised his eyebrows with resignation:

"Unfortunately, it was hard for me to state my conditions. By making my offer to the court, I simply expressed this request, which should seem reasonable: that the hostage freed in my place be, like me, a man between forty and sixty years old. Now that they've bumped off the journalist, all that's left is the liquor seller. I sent a text to my lawyer, and also to my former companion, to explain the meaning of this request; and I hope you'll repeat it, too, after my death."

"I promise you I will."

There was another silence. The two men looked at each other, inhaling their cigarette smoke; then the priest concluded:

"You'll eat something, get some rest, and then we'll leave. We have to get up early in the morning, since it's a long journey. The exchange has to take place at exactly 3 PM."

He got up in his black suit and, with the stooping walk of an old monk, led the prisoner to the dining room.

*

The next day, at the appointed time, the car stopped as planned at mile 135, in a landscape of rocks and sandy hills with bushes clinging to them. A hundred feet further on, a Mercedes from the terrorist group was waiting. Sitting in the back seat next to the priest, the prisoner felt his throat tighten. A few instants later, he was going to plunge into the violence of an absurd game. On the front seat, the militia members of Christ the King seemed impatient to get it over with. Their shoulders wide as action-film heroes, machine guns on their knees, they heaved with tubercular coughs. Despite their protests, Msgr. El Ghoury had smoked uninterruptedly since their departure, and the car's air conditioning—beneath a leaden sun—had forced them to keep the windows closed. To breathe a little fresh air, they finally opened their doors a little and made a sign to the prisoner that the time had come. He received a final embrace from the priest, then followed his guards onto the burning sand.

In cowboy hats, the terrorists walked towards them. Petrified with anguish, the voluntary prisoner moved forward like a robot. His eyes wide open, he seemed to see nothing and stumbled with every step. Finally, the two groups stopped and the guards exchanged a few words in Arabic, from a distance. Then the Christian militiamen ordered the prisoner to take twenty more steps, straight in front of him, while the freed hostage came forward from the opposite direction. The prisoner started walking again, closing his eyes, so that he could methodically count the last few feet that separated him from torture. At number ten, he stopped again to see where he was. Suddenly, as if he were recovering all his consciousness, he cried out:

"No, that's not what they promised me! I object!"

Across from him, already running towards the Christian car, he had recognized Kevin, the youngest of the hostages. The

terrorists had picked this dynamic teenager, chosen over-
whelmingly by the votes of the public, instead of the Canadian
store manager he had wanted to save. He turned around, at a
loss; but one of his Christian guards was threatening him now
with a revolver, ordering:

"Keep moving forward!"

Under the threat, he made the last few steps that separated
him from the terrorists, while continuing to shout in a
betrayed voice:

"That's not what I asked for, that's not what I said!"

A member of the group, pistol in hand, had already seized
him with his brutal grip and threw him into the car, saying, in
rudimentary English:

"We have standards, too!"

Although contrary to the prisoner's wishes, this initiative
was favorably received by public opinion. Alone in her surprise
at this betrayal, his companion published in a newspaper the
text in which he set forward the reasons for his gesture and the
choice of a hostage "of masculine sex, between forty and sixty
years old." This profession of faith contributed to tarnishing
his reputation. Some people saw a provocation in it; many people were indignant that a man suspected of a crime against
children and guaranteed a severe condemnation could claim to
dictate the choice of the victim to be saved. They had been
wrong to transform him into a hero; they congratulated themselves that the terrorists, in their abjection, showed a moral
sense of which their new prisoner seemed deprived.

Invited into TV studios as soon as he was liberated, the young Kevin was in complete agreement with the public. Far from thanking his benefactor, he said he was free of any gratitude towards a man who had done nothing to save him personally, and who had even wanted to save someone else! He added that, ever since his kidnapping, he had wanted to become a singer; in a duo with Britney from *American Idol*, he sang a song in homage to the hostages with whom he had rubbed shoulders for many weeks, especially for Françoise, the old lady who had given him "a wonderful lesson in wisdom."

During the following weeks, the course of *A Martyr Idol* underwent an unforeseen twist. In the beginning of the second round, internet users discovered that the voluntary prisoner outclassed all the others in his cleverness in the various tests. He was in the lead in the General Culture Quiz and—during the theatrical section—turned out to be particularly brilliant in the monologue from *Hamlet*. Slightly less convincing in the singing contest, he seemed however to be benefiting from a considerable number of votes—coming possibly from all those active forty- and fifty-year-olds whose defense he had taken in his testament, and who seemed to have rushed to their computers to vote.

There was a growing unease in the legal institutions. True, the prisoner had saved an adolescent's life, but they had been expecting him to keep a low profile during the game, so as not to compromise the survival of the others. It seemed tacitly understood that he would die first, as everyone waited for a possible military intervention that would free the survivors; they even hoped that other prisoners would follow his example and hand themselves over to the terrorists, allowing for the liberation of all the innocent people and transforming *A Martyr Idol* into a settling of accounts among crooks.

Foiling this hope, the prisoner held his own. From test to test, he carried the second month of competition, which resulted in the execution of the old lady—as she had requested, invoking her fatigue and the necessity of saving the younger people. The numerical weight of the world's retirees was not enough to make the scales tip in her favor; for they were less clever at handling the computer than the industrious class of active men. When, after every test, the camera came to ask the opinions of the voluntary prisoner, he invariably said the same thing. You could see his badly-shaved, ill-lit face, in the shadow of the cave that was transformed into a dressing room. Seated in an old red microfiber armchair, he explained:

"I just want to say to Latifa that I'm thinking about her, about the moments of happiness we had. Together, we tasted the pleasures of life without thinking too much about money, power, children, or brand-name clothes; we didn't feel the need to save our species or transform humanity; we knew the pleasures of good cooking and good wine, reading, the cinema, walks, and love.... And since that kind of happiness is no longer possible, now I'm almost happy to get it over with...."

During the third round, the new hostage's fate seemed less favorable. But people wondered if there weren't a deliberate reversal at stake; for an entire series of tests now pitted him against Daniel M., the former sales manager in a superstore in a suburb of Toronto. During this confrontation, it was as if the volunteer were doing all he could to spoil his own chances, despite his opponent's low intellectual level. Far from trying to impose himself, he addressed the challenger with deference:

"You know, Daniel, I don't have anything more to lose. And really, I'd be very happy if you could go back to your little house, your whisky, especially your dog...."

Not in the least touched by these suggestions, Daniel looked mistrustfully at this competitor with the strange behavior. Staring at the camera with the look of a complete idiot, he wondered out loud:

"Is this guy stupid or what?"

But the prisoner replied:

"No, Daniel, I'm not stupid. I had a dog, too; his name was Sarko and I loved him a lot. I hope he's still with my wife!"

This exchange was followed by a geography question, uttered by the group leader:

"Is Flanders in Europe, Asia, or America?"

Without hesitating, Daniel answered "Asia." His adversary seemed to think for a long time, then replied "America." Thus, from day to day, he gave the advantage to the Canadian. The two men soon had an equal number of points despite Daniel's efforts to win and his opponent's to lose. So they had to resort to another vote from the audience, and the volunteer took advantage of this to launch an appeal in favor of "Daniel who fought well, and who has the right to get his life back, his TV nights, his dog. He really has his place in the world.... Me, at the point where I am, I don't see what use I could still be." The audience, convinced, followed his advice and designated him as the loser of the third round. The group announced his execution for the following week, while Daniel explained to the camera in an aside:

"I don't really like this guy, he's weird. But I'm really happy I won today."

He held up his fist, a proud man for having fought so well.

The day of the execution coincided with Désiré's visit to Administration City. Officially received by the mayor in the early afternoon, he was to inaugurate the first *Smoking Room for Life*—a new kind of space for smokers financed by the General Tobacco Company, inside which addicted individuals could receive information, advice, and treatment so they could quit smoking. After cutting the ribbon, Désiré climbed onto the platform and walked towards the microphones accompanied by the municipal chief, followed by the lawyer Maren Pataki. He thanked the mayor for his initiative and then added:

"You see, Mr. Mayor, I haven't forgotten that I became famous because of my last cigarette. And, so that it will remain the last, I've decided to stop smoking!"

While a wave of applause rose up from the crowd, he reminded them that the only great cause, today, was saving the innocent people of *A Martyr Idol*. After making another appeal to the terrorists, he added a thought for the man whose throat would be cut that very day:

"He deserves our compassion, despite the crimes he may have committed in the past."

The mayor agreed with a sign of his head and let a few seconds of silence pass.

At the same moment, millions of internet users were trying to go online to watch the broadcast of the execution. The group leader had seized hold of the head of the prisoner, who—his terrified gaze in front of the camera—seemed to have lost his usual detachment. Remaining frozen in this theatrical attitude, as if he were posing for the television viewers, the group leader placed a long tapered knife on the victim's neck, who cried out:

"No, please...."

His plea had no effect. A few seconds passed; then the vigilante cut his hostage's neck while the blood gushed out and his body quivered like a chicken's. With the method of a sadistic surgeon, the assassin finished cutting off the head, and then held it up by the hair. Two staring eyes seemed to be asking the camera for pity.